FOUR AND TWENTY BLACKBIRDS

A WATER WITCH COZY MYSTERY - BOOK TWO

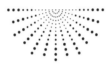

SAM SHORT

WWW.SAMSHORTAUTHOR.COM

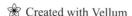 Created with Vellum

For Archie. May your life be magical.

CHAPTER ONE

*M*y sister steered the boat through the narrow gap in the trees with the skill of somebody who'd been driving sixty-foot narrow-boats for years. Nobody would have guessed it was the first time she'd attempted the tricky manoeuvre.

"Well done, Willow!" shouted Susie from the bank-side, eliciting a proud grin from my sister. "And welcome home!"

Home was a narrow dead-end channel of water which led off the canal at a tight right angle. The Poacher's Pocket Hotel, which I leased the exclusive mooring from, was hidden by trees on the hill above us, and the aroma of the guest's breakfasts being prepared made my stomach rumble. The early morning sun twinkled on the water, and an already warm breeze brushed my face as I prepared to help moor the *Water Witch* — *Floating emporium of magick.*

Willow put the gearbox into neutral as she steered the boat tight against the bank, and switched off the engine as I threw a rope to Susie. "Catch!" I dared.

My best friend snatched the rope from the air and threaded it through one of the iron hoops embedded in the thin strip of stonework that kept water and grass separate. "I can't wait to show you the shop!" she said, tying a knot and checking it was secure. "You're both going to love it!"

Willow giggled. "I'm sure we are," she said, offering me a meaningful glance.

I was happy, but my sister was at least three rungs higher than me on the excitement ladder. She'd only lived on my boat for two weeks, but the lack of her own bedroom had begun to take its toll. Willow was eighteen and needed her own space — especially when she'd run out of chocolate, and with a third of the boat's length taken up by my witchcraft shop, space was at a premium.

My sister and I had been on a two week business trip along the canals of South England, and while moored up in the quaint village of Bentbridge, on market day, we'd made a joint decision — we were going to convert the shop area into a bedroom for Willow, and take Jason Danvers up on his generous offer.

Jason had recently been accused of murder, and when Willow, Susie, and I, had helped clear his name, he'd insisted on showing us all his appreciation. Being the wealthy owner of several properties in Wickford, and eager to turn over a new leaf, Jason had offered Susie an apartment free of rent, and Willow and I the shop premises directly below it.

The temptation of paying no rent had been hard to resist, but we'd all insisted that we would only accept his offer if he took half of the rent from us each month — a deal which Jason had reluctantly agreed to.

"Just think," said Susie, tying the final boat rope to a hoop. "I'll be living above your shop, and your boat is only a two minute walk away! It's almost like living next door to each other."

I opened my mouth to answer, but a loud barking from the tree-line interrupted me. "Mabel!" I shouted, as the white goose sprinted across the grass towards us, wagging her tail feathers and flapping her wings.

A medical condition prevented her from flying, but the fact she thought she was a dog was down to an accidental spell being cast on her. My grandmother had developed a bad case of witch dementia, and Mabel had been the first victim of Granny's muddled up spells. She'd continue thinking she was a dog until Granny found a cure for her dementia, although it seemed the goose was perfectly happy with her canine lifestyle.

I patted and tickled the yapping goose as she leapt at my legs, and Rosie jumped off the boat to greet her with a happy mewl. The black cat had once been afraid of Mabel, but after finally sticking up for herself, she was now the dominant animal. Mabel allowed Rosie to sniff her face, and the two of them ran across the grass together, Mabel picking up a stick, and Rosie making an athletic leap in a failed attempt to swat a colourful butterfly from the sky.

"I've missed this," I said, hugging Susie. "It's good to be home."

The peaceful vibe was rudely ruined by a bang so loud it made my stomach flip. Susie went rigid in my arms, and my sister screamed. Mabel barked, and Rosie streaked over the grass and leapt aboard the boat, disappearing down the steps into my bedroom as another bang echoed around the clearing. Crows rose from the fields beyond the hedgerow on the other side of the canal, and a man shouted, his voice barely audible above the noise of the angry birds. "Get off my crops! I'll kill every last one of you if I have to!"

"He's shooting!" yelled Willow, leaping ashore and crouching behind the steel hull of the *Water Witch*.

Another bang proved my sister correct, but it seemed the shooter's aim was becoming less proficient as shot gun pellets snapped through the hedge and peppered the water next to the boat.

"Stop shooting!" yelled Susie, as more crows joined the circling mass of birds in the sky. "You're going to hurt somebody!"

Susie and I lowered ourselves behind one of the two picnic benches a few feet away from the waters edge, and Mabel joined us, shaking with anxiety. I placed a calming hand on her back, and she relaxed a little, lowering herself onto her tail, her orange feet stretched out in front of her in a position that would have been comical under any other circumstances.

The man shouted again. This time speaking to us and not the birds. "Hello?"

"Over here!" I yelled, "across the canal! You almost hit us!"

Cracking twigs and shaking leaves pinpointed his position as he fought his way through the hedge and stumbled onto the towpath on the opposite bank. He lifted his flat cap and shielded his eyes from the sun as he pointed the barrel of his gun safely at the ground. "Are you all okay?" he said, glancing nervously through the gap in the trees.

Willow stood up, wiping dirt from her knees and adjusting her shorts. "Yes, luckily for you," she said, raising her voice as the crows continued to register their annoyance. "You shouldn't be shooting so close to a public footpath, even I know that. The police will take your gun licence away if they catch you."

"It's Gerald Timkins," said Susie, tightening the ponytail in her long blond hair.

I'd recognised him too. The land he'd been shooting on was his, but that was still no excuse for nearly putting holes in one of us, or my boat.

"The crows are causing havoc this year," explained Gerald, breaking the barrel of his shotgun open and making me feel a little safer. "They've devastated one of my fields already."

"Get a scarecrow," shouted Willow. "You'll have more than failed crops to worry about if you carry on shooting that thing so close to a public footpath."

"I've got a scarecrow," said Gerald. "In fact, I've got two of the buggers — fat lot of good that they do. The crows just sit on them. They're going on the bonfire! I bought three of those electronic scarecrows last week — the ones that make bangs every few minutes, they're being delivered today, then maybe I can get some peace. I can hear those crows in my blasted dreams!"

The crows *were* loud, and I imagined a flock the size of the one that circled above us would make short work of a field of wheat, or whatever crop it was that Gerald grew.

The red faced farmer continued his rant. "I've got the bird watching brigade on me too, telling me I shouldn't shoot the crows. Bloody twitchers! I'd like to see what they'd say if it was *their* livelihood being eaten by the buggers!"

"I'm sorry you've got crow trouble, Mr Timkins," I said, "but can you try and be more careful in the future? I really don't like the thought of being shot, and I only had my boat painted a few weeks ago!"

Gerald nodded. "Of course," he said, "but do me a favour, girls? Don't go reporting me to the police, will you? I've got enough problems on my plate with these crows without the law sniffing around too."

None of us were the type of person to go running to the law because of an accident, and nobody had been harmed, although I had an awful feeling that a few crows wouldn't be seeing another sunrise. "We won't," I promised. "You have my word."

Gerald thanked us with a wave of his cap, and fought his way back through the hedge as the crows continued to chastise him.

"Nothing like a little excitement first thing in the morning to get the blood flowing," said Susie.

Willow smiled. "I'm ready for more. Come on, Susie, show us our shop!"

CHAPTER TWO

"Where's Jason?" I asked as Susie fished a large bunch of keys from her jeans pocket. "He said he wanted to be here when we saw inside the shop for the first time."

Susie opened the door and stood aside, letting me and Willow enter before her. "He was called away to a fire," she said, "but I'll show you around, and he said he'll be back as soon as he can."

"Called away to a fire?" I asked. The last time I'd seen Jason he'd been released from police custody after being suspected of murder. Why he'd been called to a fire was anyone's guess.

"He volunteered as a part-time fireman," explained Susie. "It seems he meant it when he said he wanted to do good with his life from now on."

All thoughts of Jason fighting fires faded as I

looked around the room which was soon going to be my shop. The space was perfect. It had been a VHS rental shop until recently — when the elderly couple who'd owned it had begrudgingly admitted that the bottom had fallen out of the market, and retired to a new home in Portugal. The shelves which had once housed videos would be perfect for wands, cauldrons, and spells, and the service counter still had an old fashioned metal till on top of it. It made a pleasant ringing sound as I opened it, and I promised myself I'd never change it for a modern beeping electronic model. It fitted in perfectly with the vision I had of how the shop would look when it was decorated and filled with stock.

The path down to my mooring ran alongside the right-hand side of the shop, and adjoining it on the left was the *Firkin Gherkin* greengrocers, which would be invaluable in helping persuade me to eat a healthy lunch each day. The Golden Wok Chinese restaurant and takeaway was opposite, and the smell of fried onions was already heavy in the street even though it wasn't quite nine o'clock in the morning. I'd eaten there once, and had vowed never to repeat the experience after discovering that Dennis, the chef, used microwavable rice and jars of shop bought sauces to make his underwhelming offerings.

The entrance to Susie's flat was a set of steps at the rear of our building, which led up to a balcony and a bright red door. The balcony was decorated with colourful plants in pots and overlooked the canal a few hundred metres away. If you leaned out over the stone wall and craned your neck, you could just make out the bow of the *Water Witch* in her mooring.

Willow span on the spot pointing at shelves and cubbyholes. "We'll put the goblets on that shelf, and the cauldrons below," she enthused. "The crystals can go on the shelf near the window where they'll catch the sun, and we can set up a table to make potions on! It's perfect!"

Susie gave a giggle and a wide grin. "I knew you'd love it," she said. "And I've got some good news of my own too." She opened her bag and retrieved a badge. "It's a press pass," she beamed, holding it up for us to inspect. "The Herald liked the work I sold them during the Sam Hedgewick case, and they offered me a position as a journalist! I can work from home, right above you two! No more free-lancing for me — I've got a job!"

Mine and Willow's excited congratulations were cut short by the ringing of the bell above the door as it opened. The bell made a sound a lot louder than the till, but not loud enough to ever become an annoyance.

"Hello!" said a big man, filling the doorway with his bulk. "I was hoping you could tell me what time the greengrocers opens. There's no sign in the window, and I'm desperate for some celery." He rubbed his almost spherical belly with a big hand. "I'm starving!"

I didn't like to say it, and I even felt guilty for thinking it, but starving was not an adjective I'd have used for the man. His stomach reached us a full foot and a half before the rest of his body as he closed the door and shuffled into the shop, and his t-shirt cast doubt on his claim he was a fan of celery. '*I ate all the pies!*' it proudly proclaimed, beneath a cartoon image of a pie, and '*South of England pie eating champion 2015,*' was emblazoned below.

He smiled as the three of us read his t-shirt. "And twenty-fourteen, *and* sixteen," he offered, with more than a hint of pride in his voice, "but they didn't do a t-shirt at last year's competition, they found better sponsors and commissioned an oil painting of me instead. It's in my bedroom, above the bed. The wife hates it, she says it stops her from falling asleep, but it makes me feel safe. The artist captured the crumbs in my beard perfectly."

I narrowed my eyes. His full black beard was currently crumb free, and it appeared to have been combed. It was a pretty nice beard all round, as beards went.

"Allow me to introduce myself," he continued, his voice remarkably high-pitched for such a large man, but then again, his jeans did seem to be constrictive in the groin area. "I'm Felix Round."

Willow opened her mouth to speak, but Felix interrupted her. "I know what you're going to say," he declared. "Round by name, round by nature! I hear it all the time!"

"Erm, no," said Willow. "I was going to tell you the greengrocers opens at quarter-past nine."

"Oh," said Felix, looking dejected. "I bet you want to know why I'm so desperate for celery though, don't you? Come on admit it! Look at the size of me... why would I be eating celery? One of you must want to know!"

Willow had the least tact. "I am slightly intrigued," she admitted. "Although I'm guessing it's because you're on a diet?"

Felix smiled and shook his head. "Incorrect! It's not a diet — it's my secret weapon," he boasted. "I only eat celery for two days before a pie eating contest. I've almost collapsed from hunger in the past, but it does the job — I'll be half dead from starvation by the time the pies are placed in front of me, and I will smash them! I'm aiming to eat nineteen this year!"

"But the contest isn't for *four* days," said Susie. "You can't live on celery for that long. *I* couldn't live on celery for that long."

It was the first I'd heard of a pie eating contest,

but I supposed it hadn't been top of Susie's list of things to tell me about when I'd arrived back in Wickford.

Felix frowned. "I'm forced to extend two days to four days. I must be strong. Dark times are upon us," he said, lowering his voice. "Rumour has it that The Tank is coming out of retirement after a three year break. I'm going to need to be extra hungry if I want to beat that bruiser."

"The Tank?" I said.

He moved nearer to us, and I took the opportunity to take a closer look at his beard. Definitely no crumbs.

"The Tank," he confirmed with a nod. "Winner of the South England pie eating contest for three years running. He once ate twelve meat and potato pies, *and* six lamb and mint — in forty-six minutes and twelve seconds. I need to be running on empty if I'm to be in with a chance of beating him. If I win this year I'll beat his record. So celery it is... for now." He fell silent for a moment and narrowed his eyes. "Then I will dominate!" he shouted, his belly wobbling and his voice trembling as it rose in volume. "The tank will wish he'd choked on the last pie he ate. I'll send him back to whatever dark corner of the county he's crawled out of and I'll fu—"

"What's going on here?" said a loud male voice. "Are you girls okay?"

Felix's shouting had disguised the sound of the bell ringing as the door opened, and Jason Danvers stood in the doorway. His tight fire brigade t-shirt moulded itself to his bulging muscles, and the soot on his face was as black as the tattoos which covered his arms. Granny had once or twice referred to him as a badboy, and he certainly looked bad as he leapt into action, taking long strides through the shop with the obvious intent of stopping Felix committing whatever heinous act Jason imagined he was about to.

Felix whimpered, and I stepped between the two men. "It's okay!" I said, placing a hand on Jason's chest. "He was just telling us a story, he got himself over excited."

"It's hunger pangs," said Felix, shrinking under Jason's gaze. "I get a little edgy when I'm hungry. The doctor said I've developed diabetes, but you can't trust the quacks, can you? What can one little blood test really tell a doctor about the intricate workings of the human body? I was told I wouldn't see Christmas twenty-ten if I didn't cut down on yak's milk, but look at me. I'm still here, and as strong as an ox!"

The door opened again, and in hurried a short thin woman with a scowl on her face, bright green polish on her fingernails, and a hairdo so large it bounced as she walked. "Felix, what on earth are you doing?" she said, taking the big man by the hand. "You only came in to ask what time the shop next door opens. I've been sitting in the car waiting for you."

"Sorry, darling," said Felix. "The young ladies were interested in hearing about the pie eating contest. You know how I like to talk."

Felix dwarfed his wife, and she sighed as she turned her husband towards the door. "Nobody wants to hear about your wretched competition, Felix. And I wish you wouldn't wear that t-shirt everywhere. It's not clever to show off about giving yourself heart disease and diabetes."

"I don't have heart disease," protested Felix, as he followed his wife. "And as you know, sweetheart, I'm dubious about the diabetes diagnosis."

His wife sighed. "I do wish you'd listen to the doctor, Felix. I'm worried sick about you, and you don't seem to care!"

"Look," said Willow, pointing through the window and relieving the tension. "It's Mr Jarvis. He owns the greengrocers. Go and get your celery, Felix, and we wish you luck in the competition. We'll be rooting for you."

I considered relieving the tension even further by pointing out Willow's possible pun, but I wasn't quite sure if celery *was* a root vegetable or not.

"Celery?" said Jason, watching the oddly matched couple leave the shop.

"Long story," I said, as the door closed behind them.

Jason wiped his forehead with the back of his hand. "I've got a story too," he said. "A story which I think you'll want to hear."

CHAPTER THREE

Willow carried a large glass of water from the small kitchen in the rear area of the shop, and Jason drank it with long thirsty gulps. He wiped his mouth with the back of a hand and leaned against the serving counter, sweat beading on his forehead.

"That fire I just got called to," he said, "was strange."

"Strange?" I said. "In what way?"

Jason took a breath and looked at us in turn. "Some thugs rolled a burning car over a cliff in the quarry. Luckily someone was walking his dog and reported it, or the fire would have spread to the trees."

"Idiot kids," said Susie. "Probably from Coven-hill. I'd hate to think we have young adults like that in Wickford."

"That's not what was strange," Jason said. "What was strange is that a goat wearing a balaclava came galloping out of the trees and attacked the firemen, me included."

"A goat?" said Willow casually.

Jason nodded. "Yes, a goat. A goat which I'm almost certain is the same goat that attacked me on your boat."

"I thought you said it was wearing a balaclava?" I said, mentally piecing together the jigsaw of what had happened in the quarry that morning, and it wasn't a difficult puzzle to put together. "How can you be sure?"

The goat *had* to be Boris — another animal which had fallen foul of Granny's witch dementia. The goat wasn't *actually* a goat — well, the body was, but the mind was that of certified acupuncturist Charleston Huang, which had accidentally been transferred into the animal. Charleston Huang was quite happy being trapped in the goat, and his body, along with the mind of the *actual* goat, was languishing in a form of magical stasis in Granny's guest bedroom, beneath her most expensive summer duvet.

Granny had promised she was going to burn Charlestons's car when she'd thought the police were looking for him. It seemed she'd followed through on her promise, and had enlisted the help of Boris.

Jason looked at me with amusement playing on

his face. "Really?" he said. "Are you trying to tell me that a balaclava wearing goat which attacked me today, isn't the same got which attacked me on your boat?"

"Maybe," said Susie. "Plenty of people keep goats, Jason. It's really not unusual, especially in rural areas of the country."

Jason narrowed his eyes and licked his lips. "Talking goats?"

Susie had no answer.

"Not this again," I said. "The police told you that was all in your imagination. When the goat bit you... down there, you hallucinated because of the pain you were in — you imagined the goat had spoken to you."

Susie and Willow nodded their agreement, though both of them knew full well that Boris had indeed hurled insults at Jason before he'd dragged him from his hiding place on my boat.

"That doesn't explain today," said Jason, shaking his head. "He spoke to me again. I know he did! He called me a 'diabolical yellow helmeted moron.' I had to take my helmet off and hit him with it to stop him biting through my water hose."

I laughed. At least I'd tried to laugh, but it came out as a snort. "Smoke inhalation," I proclaimed. "It has to be. You breathed in too much smoke and imagined the goat was talking."

Jason raised his eyebrows. "What is it with that

goat?" he said, "and what is it you're hiding from me?"

"Nothing," I said. Certainly not the fact that Willow and I were Witches, along with everyone else in my family. "You've overheated, Jason. Come on, I'll sign the rental contract for the shop and then you can go home and lie down. You look like you need a long shower and a rest."

Jason nodded. "The animal welfare people are out looking for the goat anyway. They say he could suffocate if they don't find him soon and remove the balaclava."

Willow and I swapped glances as I signed the paperwork for Jason, and my sister whispered in my ear as Jason took his empty glass into the kitchen. "So, Granny and Boris are arsonists now?" she said. "Do you think we should go and find out what's going on?"

****

Willow and I locked the shop up and said goodbye to Jason and Susie — refusing the offer of a lift from both of them, and began the walk to Granny's cottage. Ashwood cottage was high on a hill to the west of Wickford, and Willow and I took deep breaths as we climbed the steep and narrow country lane that led us there.

Birds sang and bees buzzed, and I smiled to myself as the sun warmed my face. Only Willow grabbing my arm with fingers that dug deep into my flesh, dragged me from my happy daze. "Watch out!" she screamed, as she pulled me into the hedge alongside her.

The loud roar of an engine was followed by a flash of red as a large pickup truck sped past, barely avoiding us as we squeezed ourselves against the prickles of the hedgerow. The pick-up came to a screeching halt, and the smell of burnt rubber and diesel smoke hung in the air, filling the narrow lane with toxic fumes and masking the pleasant scent of wild flowers.

A man leaned out of the driver's window and waved at us. "I'm so sorry, girls!" he shouted. "Are you both okay?"

"We're fine," I said, brushing twigs from my short red summer dress, and checking my Doctor Martens for scuffs. "Just watch where you're going in the future."

He leaned further out of the window, his blond hair and thin face barely visible through the cloud of smoke the engine spewed out. "Will do," he said. "You have my word."

His word didn't seem to count for much. He sped away with a squeal of rubber and a scream from the engine, and as he rounded the next bend, some of the loose load in the back of his vehicle spilled over the tailgate and onto the sun warmed tarmac. Neither

Willow or I had any requirement for a pile of straw and a few ragged t-shirts, so we kicked the straw off the road and carried the t-shirts with us, throwing them in the rubbish bin at the bottom of one of the farm tracks that led off the lane. Our good deed for the day.

The walk to Granny's house left Willow and I hot and sweaty, and I began to think that Mum had a valid point when she continually insisted I needed a car. Especially since I'd decided to move my shop off the boat and into a proper property. I decided to put it at the top of my list of priorities.

The lean-to attached to the side of Granny's bright yellow cottage was suspiciously devoid of wood. It *had* been stacked high with freshly cut timber which had concealed Charleston Huang's car, but the logs had been scattered, and fresh tyre marks indicated a vehicle had recently been moved. Willow and I needed no more evidence to prove that it had been Boris and Granny who were guilty of arson that morning. Not that we'd had any doubts in the first place.

The fact that a balaclava wearing goat had been on the scene was not just more damning evidence, but was also proof that Boris and Granny had not only broken the law, but were both stepping teasingly close to the line which separated them from being *relatively* normal — or a pair of raving lunatics.

Granny's front door was unlocked, and Willow and I entered the cottage to complete silence. The kitchen, which Granny spent most of her time in, was empty, and Boris was not in the study where he could often be found writing his blog and drinking brandy.

"Granny!" shouted Willow. "Are you here?"

Hurried footsteps sounded on the ceiling above us, and Granny's face appeared at the top of the narrow stairway, her blue rinse perm recently coloured, and her finger over her lips as she hushed us. "As happy as I am to see you both again, would you keep the noise down, please? Boris and I are *trying* to have a candlelit vigil."

"A candlelit vigil?" I said. "What on earth are you having —"

Granny shushed me with a hiss of air through her teeth. "It's Charleston's birthday," she whispered. "Boris and I wanted to pay our respects. If you two can keep those flapping mouths of yours quiet, you can come up and join us. Boris would appreciate it, I'm sure."

Willow looked at me and shrugged. "Candlelit vigil it is," she whispered.

Granny waited at the top of the stairs for us, and we followed her quietly to the guest bedroom. She ushered us into the dimly lit small room, and Willow's giggle elicited a stern stare from Granny.

"It's not funny!" she warned. "Boris is taking this very seriously!"

Boris sat on his haunches with his front hooves on the bed. His head was bowed and he mumbled incoherently under his breath. He looked up at us, and the tea-light candle on the bedspread in front of him almost set alight the long hairs of his beard. Small strands of black wool were visible on his horns, and his white hair was darker than usual — almost as if he'd been near a sooty fire in *very* recent history. "It's good to see you both again," he said in a low voice. "I'm sure we'll catch up later, but for now, please light a candle each and join Gladys and I in celebrating the end of another year in the life of a remarkable man."

"And the beginning of another," murmured Granny, gazing at the acupuncturist who lay in her guest bed.

Only Charleston Huang's head was visible, resting on two plumped up pillows which were scattered with rose petals. The petals matched the colour of the rose plants climbing up the outside walls of Granny's cottage, and tiny aphids crawled off them and onto the white linen pillowcases.

The rest of Charleston's body was covered by a flower print duvet, and his face still wore the shocked expression it had adopted when Granny's witch dementia had switched his mind with that of a goat.

His mouth was frozen in a perfect O shape, but his eyelids had been closed — by Granny, I presumed. I tried convincing myself that he looked peaceful, but if I was being brutally honest with myself — he looked like a man who'd been jabbed in the buttock with a long and very sharp pin.

Charleston's body was in complete magical stasis, and the mind of the goat trapped in it was oblivious to anything that was happening. Until Granny cured her witch dementia, the minds could not be switched back, and even then, it was doubtful that Charleston would want his mind to be put back in his own body. He'd become strangely accustomed to living life in the body of a goat, and had insisted that people called him Boris, out of respect for the goat whose body he inhabited.

Willow passed me a candle, and I lit it using the lighter which Granny offered me. Granny had never had a cigarette lighter in the house until she'd moved the goat in with her, but Boris was fond of cigars, and brandy — in large quantities.

Granny peered over her purple glasses. "Kneel down, girls," she said. "Join Boris in his tribute. I'll remain standing. Boris has given me special dispensation due to an injury I acquired this morning... while... feeding the chickens."

"Not while pushing a burning car over a cliff in a quarry?" mumbled Willow, as she lowered herself next to Boris and joined him in his solemnity. Willow had never learned to let Granny's lies go unchallenged.

The candle in Granny's hand dropped to the floor at her slipper clad feet, and she broke the dignified silence with a gasp. "I don't know what you mean! And neither does Boris! Car? Burning? Cliff? None of those words make any sense!" Granny's face paled, and she slowly lowered herself to her knees and crumpled into a heap on the carpet, wrapping her arms around herself. "Nothing happened at the quarry this morning," she mumbled. "I was feeding the chickens. Nothing happened at the quarry."

Her whimpers turned to sobs, and her eyes glazed over, adopting the expression which Willow and I recognised as her thousand-yard-stare. Granny had temporarily shut down.

"Gladys?" said Boris, his face looking convincingly concerned for a goat. "Gladys!" He leapt to his feet, sending wax flying as his beard knocked his candle over. The wax flew in hot arcs which splattered the duvet and the already shocked face of the Chinese acupuncturist in the bed. "Gladys!" he repeated, tapping her with a hoof. "Oh, Gladys! Where have you gone?"

"She's shut down, Boris," I said placing a hand on his back. "It's nothing to worry about, I'm surprised this is the first time you're seeing it, if I'm honest. *Really* surprised."

"Poor Gladys," said Boris. "The shock of what we were forced to do this morning has evidently caught up with her."

"You mean burning a car?" said Willow.

Boris looked into Granny's glassy eyes. "It was necessary. It's my body's birthday, and Gladys and I wanted to begin the next year with a fresh start. Having my car hidden away in the lean-to was just too much of a problem for the both of us. It's only a matter of time before somebody notices Charleston is missing — even though I've been spreading false information over the internet that he's gone away on a vacation. Imagine if they found my body here in magical stasis — your family secret would be revealed to the world before you could say abra-cadabra."

He was right of course. The fact that my family were witches was a secret known only to a few people, and none of us wanted anybody else finding out. "I can understand you burning the car," I said, "but attacking the firemen was inexcusable."

Granny groaned. "That wasn't Boris," she mumbled, snapping out of her shock induced trance. "It was another goat."

Even Boris rolled his eyes.

"So, you're telling us that there was another goat

who just happened to be in the quarry at the same time as you two were there?" said Willow, helping Granny to her feet with a hand under her arm.

"A balaclava wearing goat which attacked the firemen?" I added. I picked a strand of wool from one of Boris's horns and held it out for Granny to inspect.

"Good grief, Boris!" said Granny. "You just can't hide evidence very well at all, can you?" She sat on the bed, her bottom inches from Charleston's wax splattered face. It seemed that the dignified vigil was well and truly over. "It's your fault we had to send you after the firemen, and now your leaving evidence on your horns! Remind me not to involve you in anything potentially illegal again. You're a liability!"

"Why was it Boris's fault?" I asked.

Granny straightened her glasses. "He said there was nothing with his name on in the car. *Until* the fire brigade arrived and began putting the fire out. *Then* he remembered his passport was in the glove compartment. We had to make sure that car burnt to the ground! I'd been up all night filing the identification numbers off the chassis and engine, and then that daft goat goes and leaves his passport in it! It was imbecilic of him."

"So you sent Boris to distract the firemen until the car was completely burnt out and all the evidence was destroyed," I said. "And you just happened to have a balaclava with you? I'm not even going to ask why you thought it was necessary to make Boris wear it. He's a goat for goddess's sake!"

"Boris is a very distinguished and easily recognisable goat," said Granny, "especially since he won the beautiful farmyard animal competition, and I've always got a balaclava in my bag. You never know when you'll stumble upon a protest. I've needed that balaclava more often than the lipstick I carry in the same bag."

Granny had very rigid political views which had landed her in trouble in the past. It was no shock to me or Willow that she carried a means of hiding her face with her at all times.

"Be warned," I said. "The animal welfare people are searching for Boris, and you'd better hope the police don't find out who the car belongs to."

Granny stood up, bent over Charleston, and began peeling dried wax from his face. "Bah!" she laughed. "The policeman who turned up at the fire was your friend Barney. Forgive me if I say I'm not particularly nervous about the possibility of being found out."

"That's not fair," I said. "Barney did well during the Sam Hedgewick murder investigation."

"Rubbish!" scoffed Granny, gathering up the petals from the pillows. "We all know it wasn't Barney who solved that murder, and I'll go to the foot of my stairs if Barney Dobkins manages to even work out it was a car that was set on fire, let alone link it to me or Boris."

Granny snapped her head upright as a loud knocking on the front door echoed through the cottage. "Who on earth could that be?" she said. "It can't be Maggie, she's preparing for a visitor, and it's certainly not the window cleaner. The cast isn't due to be taken off his leg for another three weeks, and he seemed sincere when he said he'd never clean my windows again. Strange though — most young men would be happy to be confronted by a pair of bare breasts when they reached the top of a ladder. He must bat for the other team… that's the only rational explanation."

There were so many questions to ask, starting with who was visiting my mother, and then moving swiftly onto Granny's indecent exposure incident. Willow prevented me from asking them though, as she moved the curtain aside and looked through the window. "It's Barney," she said, "and he's wearing his uniform. It looks like he's here on official police business."

CHAPTER FOUR

*T*he knocking on the front door grew louder, and Granny pointed to the bedroom door. "Code red! Everybody downstairs!" she panicked. She closed the door behind us as we paraded along the landing. "Boris!" she ordered, "you go straight out of the back door and into the garden, it's time for you to pretend you're a garden goat."

We rushed down the stairs, and Granny pointed to Boris's study. "Willow, it's your job to go in there and make it look like it's not a room that a goat uses to get drunk and write a blog in." She looked at me. "Penny, it's your job to keep Barney's mind occupied. It's obvious he's got the hots for you, and it's time for you to use that to your advantage. We can't let him find Charleston."

As Boris trotted through the house and out of the

back door, Willow began work in Boris's study, moving empty brandy glasses and hiding ashtrays. Granny nodded appreciatively at Willow's efforts and put a wide smile on her face as she opened the front door. I stood next to her and smiled at Barney as he gazed down at us. "Penny, you're home!" he said, with a twinkle in his eyes.

The last time I'd seen Barney I'd promised him that we'd go out for a meal together, and I thought that in the circumstances it wouldn't be too manipulative of me to use the arrangement as a means of distraction. Even I knew that it would be no good for any of us if Barney was to discover the magically frozen body of Charleston Huang in Granny's guest bedroom. I could put my principles aside for the time being.

Not used to the intricacies of flirting, I imagined what Willow would do in my position, and pushed my chest out a little as I widened my smile. "Hi, Barney," I gushed. "It's so good to see you. I'm really excited about going out for that meal with you. Did you come here looking for me?"

"Really?" said Barney, his cheeks blushing a deep crimson. "I mean yes. I mean no. I mean I'm looking forward to taking you out, but I'm not here for that."

"Well, just what are you here for, young man?" snapped Granny. "I hope you haven't come here to try and take down *my* particulars."

Barney looked at his feet. His trouser legs exposed far too much of the shiny black leather of his boots, and his stab jacket hung from his skinny frame. He politely removed his hat, revealing his neatly combed ginger hair, and gave Granny a nervous smile. "I am here on duty, Mrs Weaver," he said sheepishly. "But I'm confident there's been a mistake. If I could just clear a few things up, I'm sure I can be on my way."

Granny gazed up at Barney's face, her neck clicking as she struggled to find the correct angle. She shielded the sun from her eyes with a hand, and sighed. "And what things might they be, PC Dobkins? Have I been reported for shouting at that machine in the convenience store again? It keeps telling me I've got an unexpected item in the bagging area. What am I supposed to do? Reason with it? I'll shout at that machine until it finds some manners, and nobody will tell me otherwise!"

Barney shook his head. "No," he said. "No one's complained about that *this* week. I'm here because of an incident that occurred this morning. In the quarry."

"What happened?" I said, hoping that Barney wasn't very good at reading body language. I relaxed my face a little, and gave him another smile.

"There was a fire," said Barney. "A car was set alight, and people normally only set fire to cars when they've got a crime to hide."

Granny grew an inch in height, her head almost level with Barney's chest. "Are you trying to say I'm a criminal?" she blasted, "because if you are, young man, I'd rather you just come right out and say it, than continue beating around the bush."

"Gosh, no!" said Barney. He'd seemed to have lost a few inches in height under the wilting stare of Granny, and he took a half step backwards along the garden path, almost tripping over his feet. "Sergeant Cooper sent me, he's received reports of an elderly woman spotted near the scene, and with the addition of a masked violent goat, I think he's put two and two together and thought that maybe… just maybe, it had something to do with you and that goat you keep in your garden."

Granny placed one of her hands behind her back, and I knew without looking there'd be sparks flying from her fingertips. I couldn't allow Granny to cast any spells, not only because of the danger her witch dementia posed to Barney and anybody else within ten metres, but also because I liked Barney, and I knew Granny did too — she was just panicking.

Granny flinched as I placed a calming hand on her shoulder, but the tension left her muscles. "Elderly!" she said. "Do I look elderly to you, Barney Dobkins?"

"Of course not, Mrs Weaver!" said Barney. "The witness said the suspect had blue hair too, maybe that's why Sergeant Cooper thought of you. You don't look a day over seventy to me."

Granny made a low growling sound in her throat, and I shook my head at Barney with my eyes wide. He understood my message. "I mean you don't look a day over sixty, Mrs Weaver," he said.

Granny patted her hair with both hands and straightened her apron. "Thank you, Barney," she said, "that's very kind of you. I try my best, and isn't it nice to know that Penny will grow into an older woman as beautiful as I am? Good looks run in this family, so you can be assured that if the meal you're taking my granddaughter on goes well, you won't be walking around with a sunken faced old hag on your arm in forty years' time."

"Granny!" I said. "Barney's taking me out for a meal to thank me for my help during the Sam Hedgewick case! Stop embarrassing him." I raised my eyebrows in an apology to Barney. "What is it you need from Granny? I said. "I'm sure she'd be happy to clear her name."

Barney took a notepad from his pocket. "I'm really sorry I have to do this," he said, "but Sergeant Cooper will come here himself if I don't ask you these questions."

Granny sighed. "Ask away, young man, but don't you dare ask for my date of birth. A lady is entitled to *some* secrets."

Barney nodded and touched his pen to paper. "Okay," he said, "would you mind me asking where you were this morning between the hours of eight and nine o'clock, Mrs Weaver?"

Granny placed a hand on her chin and looked at the sky. "Let me think," she said, "where was I between the hours of eight and nine this morning?" She locked her eyes on Barney's. "Where do you *think* I was? I was where I always am at that time of the day! Right here, in my cottage. Next question please, police constable."

Barney scribbled in his notepad and shuffled his feet. "I'm afraid I'm going to have to ask to see your goat… Boris, isn't it?" he said. "And I just need to take a quick look around your cottage."

"What on earth do need to do all that for?" said Granny. "Have you got a warrant?"

Barney sighed. "Mrs Weaver," he said, "this is really awkward for me. I don't want to be asking these questions, and I certainly don't want to infringe on your privacy, but if I don't, Sergeant Cooper will do it himself. I was hoping you'd be more under-standing if it was me that turned up on your doorstep. I just want to be able to cross you out of my notebook and tell Sergeant Cooper you've done nothing wrong."

"Of course you can see Boris," I said, pulling Granny aside, and gesturing at Barney to come inside.

"And I'd be happy to show you around Granny's cottage. I don't know what you're looking for though."

"Burnt clothing, petrol cans, that sort of thing," said Barney. "Nothing that I'll find here, I'm positive."

Granny's eyes sparkled as her brain leapt into gear. "Take Barney into the garden and show him the goat, Penny," she said. "I'll just go and tidy up a little, it's been a long time since a man has been in my bedroom, and I want it to look nice."

"You're not going to hide something, are you?" laughed Barney. His smiling face quickly transformed into a look of fear as Granny scowled at him. "It was just a joke," he said, moving behind me.

I took him by the elbow. "Come on," I said. "I'll take you into the garden."

Granny scampered up the stairs as I led Barney through the cottage. The back door was open and I was relieved to see that Willow had overheard the conversation on the doorstep and was taking evasive action. Boris didn't look relieved though. He stood with his head bowed, shivering as Willow washed him down with the hosepipe. His beard dripped with water, but as we neared him I was happy to see that his hair was white and any evidence of sooty water had soaked into the lawn.

The chickens squawked as overspray splattered

them, and Barney stopped a few feet from Willow with a frown on his face. "Hi," he said, "washing the goat?"

Boris made a spluttering sound as Willow washed a stray strand of wool from one of his horns.

"It's a warm day, Barney," said Willow. "He was getting a little overheated."

Barney studied Boris, and Boris stared back at him, narrowing his eyes. "He does look a little aggressive," said Barney. "Are you sure he couldn't have escaped and found his own way to the quarry? Maybe some kids caught him and put a balaclava on him?"

"Of course not," said Willow. "He's tied to a pole."

Barney gave the goat one last look. "Listen," he said, speaking to both me and Willow, and wiping his brow with the back of a hand. "I know the fire was nothing to do with your grandmother, and to be honest, I wouldn't really care if it was. You two helped me with my last case, and I won't forget that. I'll just have a quick look around the cottage, tell Sergeant Cooper that he's barking up the wrong tree, and get on with my day."

"Coooeee!" came Granny's raised voice. "You can come and have a look around, Barney! Everything's in order now! There's nothing to see here!"

Granny leant from her bedroom window waving

at us, and Barney raised his eyebrows. *"Everything's in order now. There's nothing to see.* What does she mean?"

"She just means she's tidied up a little," said Willow, twisting the nozzle of the hose to the off position, much to Boris's obvious delight. He shook the water from his hair and gave a loud satisfied sigh.

"Is he alright?" said Barney. "He sounds like he needs to see a vet."

"He's perfectly okay," I said, taking Barney by the wrist and leading him down the garden path, both literally and figuratively. "Come on, you can decide which restaurant you want to take me to, while you look around Granny's cottage."

Willow followed us, and together we showed Barney around the bottom floor of the cottage. He gazed around unfazed as we took him into what had once been Granny's prized backroom, but had recently been transformed into a goat's study. Willow had done a good job of making it look almost normal. The empty glasses and half-drunk bottles of brandy had vanished, and the ash trays full of cigar ends were hidden — although the room was still rich with the scent of expensive tobacco. Boris's cushion had been turned upside down, hiding the white hairs, and his computer coffee table desk had been cleared of the technology a goat needed to navigate the internet.

Barney cleared his throat. "Thanks, girls," he said.

"I'll just have a quick walk around upstairs, and I'll be on my way."

Willow led the way up the stairs and Barney brought up the rear. "I was thinking of the Golden Wok," he said, as we neared the top, where Granny stood waiting with a smug look on her face. "If you like Chinese food that is."

"That sounds lovely," I lied.

"That way, constable!" said Granny, with her back to the closed door of the guest bedroom, pointing Barney in the direction of her bedroom and the rest of the top floor.

Barney gave an embarrassed smile and poked his head around the open door of the bathroom. "It's okay!" hissed Granny, as Barney moved into the next room. "I've hidden Charleston!"

"Where?" I said. "There's nowhere in that room to hide him, and you couldn't have fitted him under the bed!"

Granny patted me on the shoulder. "Trust me, Sweetheart. Granny knows best."

Barney emerged from Granny's bedroom. "Thank you, Mrs Weaver," he said. "If I could just look in the last room, I'll leave you to enjoy the rest of the day."

Granny swung the door to the bedroom open, and gestured at Barney to step inside. "Be my guest," she said, winking at me and Willow. "I'm sure you'll find everything is in order."

I took a deep breath as Barney stepped into the room, but the air barely had the chance to fill my lungs before Barney gave a panicked cry. "What the —" he shouted. "Who the — what's going on? Come out of there with your hands where I can see them!"

I followed Willow into the room with my heart in my mouth and my mind in slow motion. Willow came to a dead stop, and I bumped into her back as the two of us unravelled what we were seeing.

CHAPTER FIVE

*B*arney stood frozen to the spot with his nightstick raised above his head. "Come out!" he repeated, edging closer to the corner of the room.

Willow gave a choking gasp, and Granny ran into the room and put her hand on Barney's arm. "It's okay," she said. "He's a friend of the family."

Barney ignored Granny. "Come out!" he repeated. "I'm not stupid, I can see you."

The fact that Barney could see Charleston Huang in no way indicated any lack of stupidity on his behalf. When Granny had insisted she'd hidden Charleston, I'd had my doubts, but what I was looking at raised important questions about Granny's level of sanity. Or complete lack of it.

Charleston was unceremoniously propped up in

the corner, with one of Granny's spare curtains draped over him. The curtain covered him from the neck down, hanging off him like an ill-fitting moo-moo. I stared in disbelief as Barney approached Charleston and lifted a light-shade from his head, stumbling backwards as the shocked face of the acupuncturist confronted him.

Granny shrugged. "I did my best," she said. "Now, have you two girls been studying my spell book? Or do I have to attempt a spell myself, and risk turning Barney into a standing lamp?"

Barney touched Charleston's face, prodding him with a finger. "What have you done?" he said, slowly turning to face us. "Is he dead? Did you kill him? Who is he? I knew something was wrong here. I saw the tyre tracks near the lean-to, and I wondered why you were washing the goat! You've killed this man and burnt his car to hide the evidence! What's the goat got to do with all this, though? And why does it smell of cigar smoke downstairs? None of you smoke!"

"A spell would be very handy right now," said Granny, leaning against the doorframe, looking far too casual for a woman being accused of murder. "My fingers are itching to cast one, and if I cast it, who knows what will happen. My dementia's feeling very playful today."

Barney reached for his radio, and Willow raised

her hand. Purple sparks played on the fingertips, and Barney's mouth widened into an O, matching the expression which was etched on the man's face behind him. "I'm sorry, Barney," said Willow.

"Wh — what's happening here?" stammered Barney. "Am I awake?"

Barney pressed the button on his radio and Willow clicked her fingers. Barney's hands dropped to his sides and he looked around the room in confusion. "Where am I?" he said. "Penny? Willow? Mrs Weaver? Is this heaven?"

I'd have liked to have thought that heaven would have been a little more pleasant than a gloomy guest bedroom containing three witches and a frozen Chinese acupuncturist, but I supposed every mortal had their own personal vision of paradise. I was quite flattered to be included in Barney's.

"No, Barney," said Willow, "It's not heaven and everything's going to be okay. I need you to listen to me, do you understand?"

Barney nodded.

"Put the nightstick away, and pick your hat up."

Barney did as he was told, stooping slowly to retrieve his hat from the floor.

Willow continued. "You're going to walk downstairs, and when you get outside, you're going to believe that you've looked around the cottage and everything was as it should be. You'll forget about tyre tracks, goats, and men in this bedroom. Do you understand, Barney?"

Barney nodded again.

"Tell him to forget about the Golden Wok," I said. "The food there is vile."

"Do you want him to forget about taking you out for a meal completely?" offered Willow.

Barney's confused eyes settled on my face, and he lifted a hand towards me, his fingers trembling, and his voice soft as he spoke. "Penny, have you tried the duck in orange sauce? It's divine."

I smiled. "No, Willow. I'll go for a meal. I want to, just not the Golden Wok."

"Barney," said Willow, her hand at waist height. "You'll remember that Penny said she'd go for a meal with you, but you'll be adamant that she chooses where. Oh, and you'll offer to pay the whole of the bill, including drinks and any taxi fares incurred."

"Half," I said.

"You'll go dutch, Barney," said Willow. She winked at me. "Very modern of you, Penny."

"Can you ask him to ignore any complaints from the window cleaner?" asked Granny. "I'm sure he's the type to try his luck at getting compensation from me."

Willow glared at Granny. "You deserve to pay more than just the window cleaner compensation, and

I don't want to hear any more about that whole sorry saga. Some things are best left to the imagination."

"I'll let you keep my spell book for as long as you need it?" pleaded Granny.

Willow and I had acquired Granny's treasured spell book using manipulation and blackmail. It was fittingly appropriate that Granny was now using it as a means to manipulate Willow.

I tried for a better deal. "And let us use your car until I buy one?" I said.

Granny waved a casual hand. "You can have that old thing. Boris is buying us a new one. He wants us to have one of those big Range Rovers."

Charleston Huang was a wealthy man, and Boris had already allowed Granny to use his credit card. It came as a mild surprise that he'd let Granny buy a new car though, especially one that pricey.

"Deal?" I asked Willow.

"Deal," she confirmed. She waved her hand at Barney. "If a window cleaner approaches you with allegations of indecent exposure —"

"Accidental exposure," corrected Granny.

"Of any sort of exposure," continued Willow. "You're to ignore him and tell him to drop any insurance claims against Granny."

Barney nodded, his eyelids drooping. "Indecent. Granny. Understood," he slurred.

"Everyone got what they wanted?" said Willow.

Granny and I both agreed.

"Okay, Barney," said Willow. "Walk downstairs, open the front door, and when you turn to face us, everything will be as it should be, and you'll think everything I've asked you to do is all your own idea."

Barney nodded slowly, dragging his feet as he made his way past us and down the stairs. We followed him closely with Willow directly behind him, sparks still crackling from her fingers.

Sunlight poured into the hallway as Barney opened the heavy front door, and the moment he stepped over the threshold his whole posture changed. He stopped for a few seconds, rolling his shoulders and taking a deep breath, before turning slowly on the spot to face us.

Willow dropped her hand and the sparks disappeared as Barney rubbed his eyes and blinked a few times. "Sorry to have disturbed you, Mrs Weaver," he said, putting his hat on. "I was only doing my job, I hope you understand."

"And a fine job you did too, Barney," said Granny. "Most thorough indeed. It makes me feel safe to know that the constabulary employs officers of such high calibre."

"Just serving my community," beamed Barney. "It's an honour."

"Off you trot then," suggested Granny. "I've got

things to do, and you've taken up enough of my time already today."

Barney straightened his hat and pulled his trousers up, showing a flash of white sock above his boots. "Let me know when you've decided on a restaurant, Penny," he said.

I gave him my sincerest smile. "I will," I promised.

"I've got a better idea," said Granny.

I doubted it, but I let her speak.

"My son's arriving for a visit today, Barney." she said. "He's coming to watch the pie eating competition. He loves a nice pie, does Brian. He's staying at Maggie's cottage and we're having a family meal tonight to welcome him and make him feel safe. He's oppressed you see, and he'd love it if an officer of the law was present."

So that's who Mum had been preparing the cottage for. My uncle Brian, her brother. Oppressed though? Uncle Brian was the least oppressed person I knew. Apart from Granny, of course. "I'm sure Barney doesn't want to spend his Friday evening with us," I said, scowling at my grandmother. "He's got better things to do, and anyway, Willow and I weren't asked if we wanted to attend a meal, and Uncle Brian is *not* oppressed."

Granny wiped her hands on her apron and forced her glasses to the top of her nose. "Until the day there's a gay astronaut — Brian is, and will remain, oppressed. And I'm telling you two girls right now that you're coming to Maggie's meal. You haven't seen her for two weeks. She's preparing a feast, *and* she's using her best porcelain. The set with the little blue and white Chinese folk on it."

Barney cleared his throat. "I'd love to come, Mrs Weaver," he said diplomatically. "It would be a pleasure to meet your son, and Maggie *does* know how to cook."

It wouldn't be the first time Barney had been to my mum's for a meal. Last time, she'd cooked lasagne, and she'd glowed for hours after Barney had enthusiastically praised her cooking skills. The ingredients had come from the haven though, and anything cooked with ingredients brought back from the haven was always going to taste good. The magical dimension was off limits to Willow and I until we'd acquired enough magic skills to be given our entry spells, but rumour had it that mine was to be given to me in the near future. If you believed my mother, and Aunt Eva — who was a permanent resident of the haven, and a renowned gossipmonger, that is.

Granny was unable to visit the haven until her witch dementia cleared up, but that was probably a good thing. Granny had caused a lot of trouble in the haven in the past, and it would do her good to stay away for a while.

"Well that clears that up!" said Granny. "Now, off you go, Barney. You need to catch an arsonist, and I need to tend to my goat. We've both got quite a day ahead of us! I look forward to seeing you at Maggie's cottage at seven o'clock sharp."

"Seven it is!" smiled Barney.

He headed down the path towards his car, and I whispered to Willow. "What spell was that?" I said. "It was very impressive."

"A spell of purged memory," said Willow. "Page twenty-four in Granny's book."

"Well done, girls," said Granny, pushing between us. "We averted a disaster back there. He's a cunning one... that Barney Dobkins. I really didn't think he'd spot Charleston. He's got eyes like a hawk and a brain built for policing, that boy!"

"You draped a curtain over Charleston and put a light shade on his head," I said. "Of course Barney saw him!"

"He'll make a fine Sergeant one day," continued Granny. "He'll clean this town up and show the criminals who's boss. You mark my words."

Barney waved at us as he opened the car door, and reached for his radio as it crackled into life. "Okay," he said, speaking quickly. "I'll be straight there. Give Mrs Oliver a cup of tea and tell her to calm down."

There's nothing more infuriating than only hearing one side of what sounds like a very important conversation, and I hated being infuriated. "What's happened?" I asked.

Barney sighed. "The same as yesterday, and the day before," he said. "Birdwatchers complaining about one of the farmers shooting crows. He's not breaking any laws, but you try and tell Mrs Oliver that."

I remembered my promise to Gerald Timkins. I didn't want to get him in trouble, so I feigned ignorance. "That sounds more exciting than looking around Granny's cottage," I said.

Barney put the car in gear and edged forward. "You haven't met Mrs Florence," he shouted through the open window.

"Seven o'clock Barney!" shouted Granny, tapping her watch. "Make sure you're there on time, Maggie's doing a prawn cocktail starter. She'll be as crazy as a dwarf in a stilt shop if you're late!"

Barney waved his acknowledgement, and Granny turned her attention to us as the police car left her property.

"I'd like you two to do me a favour," she said. "Boris is a little upset that he can't come to the meal at your mother's tonight. I'd like you to let him stay on your boat. It will lift his spirits, I'm sure."

"But we'll be at the meal," Willow said, "and I don't like the idea of Boris being alone on the boat.

Those hooves of his could cause all sorts of problems."

"Ask Susie to look after him," said Granny. "She and Boris get along like a house on fire. They'll have a wonderful time together, and it will give Susie an excuse to refuse Maggie's invitation to dinner — she said she was going to ask her."

I was absolutely sure that Susie wouldn't want to come to my mum's for a Weaver family meal, and I was absolutely certain that Granny wasn't going to take no for an answer.

"Of course he can stay on the boat," I said. "I'll phone Susie and ask her."

"Good," said Granny. "Take Boris with you as soon as you can. I need to get ready."

"Ready for what?" said Willow.

"There's a gentleman coming from the Range Rover dealership to pick me up. I'm collecting our new car. You two can take my old car and call it your own. I'll miss it, but Boris has ordered a private registration plate for the new ride, and he said the sound system is thumping. I'm rather looking forward to driving it. Boris said it will give me social mobility. I can finally say goodbye to the working-class, and hello to the lower middle-class."

"You've never worked a day in your life though, Granny," said Willow. "You can't really call yourself working-class."

I often wondered why Willow couldn't keep her mouth in the same position I kept mine when Granny made an outlandish claim — firmly closed.

Granny took a deep breath, and the sound I heard was either an animal crashing through the trees surrounding the cottage, or Granny's knuckles cracking behind her back. The look of pain on her face suggested the latter.

"Never worked?" she murmured, her voice taking on the same tone she used for the Jehovah's Witnesses who insisted on knocking her door on a Sunday, even after one of them had almost had a finger severed in a slammed door as he handed Granny a leaflet.

Granny's voice rose in volume, and Willow closed her mouth. She always got there eventually. "Never worked!" lambasted Granny. "When you've pushed two fledgling humans from the space between *your* legs, young lady, and brought them up to be well adjusted adults — while being unpaid and under appreciated... then, and only then, can you tell me I've never worked! Curses of the goddess be upon you!"

Willow's eyes glinted, and her mouth opened tentatively. I shook my head, but it was too late. "Well adjusted?" she said. "Have you had another two children you're not telling us about, or do you *actually* mean Mum and Uncle Brian?"

Granny did well to control herself. Or more likely, it was the fact that a large black saloon car turned into her driveway and parked at the bottom of the garden path which caused the sparks at her fingertips to fizzle out and die.

"My ride's here!" she said, making her way down the path. "You had a lucky escape, Willow. The keys to my car are on the kitchen table, make sure you lock the cottage when you leave and put the keys under the stone chicken."

The stone chicken stood to the right of the cottage doorway, and Granny insisted she'd bought it from a garden centre, although there was speculation that it was the chicken that Granny had insisted had been taken by a fox. The stone egg which protruded from the rear of the chicken, and the look of astonishment on its face, told a different story.

"You can't wear an apron to go and pick up a luxury car," said Willow.

Granny hurried down the path as the driver of the car opened the passenger door for her. "Like I said, I'm still working class. I'll take my apron off when I'm lower middle-class."

CHAPTER SIX

Some people might think that's it's preposterous to have a goat in the back seat of a small yellow Renault hatchback, and I was, without doubt, one of those people. It was more than preposterous — it was complete lunacy, *and* the car smelt like a petting zoo. There was hardly room in the rear of the tiny French car to seat two adults, and Boris was doing a good job of making the car seem even smaller than it actually was.

The tartan rug beneath him was managing to keep the seat fairly free of goat hair, but his rear hooves were leaving scuff marks on the plastic door trims. The window he was looking out of was smeared with tongue shaped swipes of saliva, and he bristled when I asked him to stop licking the glass.

"Penelope, you and Willow have only owned this

car for fifteen minutes, and if it wasn't for me being generous enough to buy a new car, you wouldn't own it at all," he said, tasting the glass again. "There's a small part of the goat's brain that continues to control some of my impulses, and unfortunately for you and your window, this is one of those moments. Please give me my dignity and don't mention the subject again. Anyway, when Gladys brings our new Range Rover home you won't need to transport me anywhere again. I'll be riding in style in the future, not in this embarrassingly old yellow tinpot contraption."

The car *was* old, but it held memories that made me smile. Granny had bought it when Willow and I were young enough to believe her when she'd told us that it was a top of the range sports car — the same model that Prince Charles drove when he wasn't being ferried around by his chauffeur. It had a special place in my heart, and the sound the small engine made when it struggled to climb a hill reminded me of my boat. I knew that it wasn't the best looking car on the road, and I'd agree with Boris that it was *slightly* embarrassing, but Granny had given it to me and Willow, and it was our first car. It felt special. Anyway, I didn't think it was too pernickety of me not to want goat drool on my car window.

Willow laughed. "If you can control your impulse to eat Granny's grass, and make her push that heavy lawnmower around, you can control your impulses to lick a window, Boris."

Boris snorted. "Grass tastes vile," he said. "If she wants an animal to eat her grass she can find herself another goat — one with no pride in itself. Anyway, Gladys needs the exercise. You have to keep moving when you get to a certain age or the rot begins to set in."

I laughed. "I dare you to say that to Granny's face," I said, reversing the car into a space in the Poacher's Pocket Hotel carpark, "but please let me watch."

"I have far more sense than that," said Boris, climbing out of the car. "I may be inclined to lick windows, but my faculties are just fine."

Granny had cursed people for far less than an insult about her age, and I very much doubted that she'd hold back from cursing Boris, even though he did seem to have an uncanny ability to bring out the best side in her. I'd not seen Granny treat anyone with the respect she gave Boris since my grandad had died. Boris had far more sense than to incur a curse from Granny, though — especially while she had witch dementia.

Willow led the way through the beer garden towards the path that led to the boat, and I rolled my eyes as several men stopped what they were doing and watched her progress. Her figure was what you'd call "full" and I looked down at my own body, wondering if a spell could enlarge my boobs. Willow and I shared the same black hair as my mother, and you could even say our noses were moulded from the same cast, but from the neck down, all similarities ended.

Willow's bottom *rolled* in her tight shorts, and I was sure mine wobbled, or at least bounced beneath my summer dress. The flip-flops my sister wore on her feet caused her to walk in a way that enhanced her legs, and my burgundy Doctor Marten boots just made my feet feel heavy. Maybe a shopping trip was in order. An *online* shopping trip, I promised myself as I recalled the last time I'd agreed to accompany my sister on a shopping spree. The thought of queuing for a changing cubicle with armfuls of clothes which weren't going to fit, was almost as appealing as admitting to anybody that I was quite looking forward to going out for a meal with Barney. Not that there was anything wrong with Barney, but I'd kept my life free of romantic complications for years, and the thought of the squeals and questions which would come my way from Willow and Susie if I so much as hinted that I liked Barney, made me blush.

Boris trotted ahead of me, ignoring the comments from drunk adults, and allowing children to pat and prod him. I reminded myself that beneath the coarse white hair and curled horns was a cultured man whose life had been turned upside down by Granny's dementia. I almost shed a tear of pity as Boris attempted a bleat to please a young girl who tickled him behind his ear and told him he was beautiful.

As with most things concerning Boris, the precious moment soon passed, and I almost choked on my tongue as Boris spat on the shoes of a woman who called him a mangy old animal as he brushed past her bare legs.

The woman shrieked and kicked out at Boris, and a group of men laughed as she tumbled backwards off the bench she was sitting on and sprawled on the grass, legs akimbo, and covered with the contents of her glass.

Willow placated the angry woman and helped her to her feet, taking money from her pocket to pay for the spilt drink. I ushered the angry Boris through the gate at the bottom of the garden and down the pathway which took us through the trees and down to my boat. "You are *not* a mangy old animal," I assured him. "You didn't have to spit on her shoes though, Boris. They looked very expensive."

"I did not spit," said Boris, as Willow caught up with us. "Llamas, football players, and drunk hobos spit, Penelope. I accidentally spilled a build up of fluids in my mouth. There's a huge difference! I won't be labeled uncouth by anybody, especially a witch who lives on a boat!"

"Chill out, Boris!" snapped Willow. "What on earth's got into you? I just had to pay five-pounds-fifty to buy that woman a fresh glass of Pimms. Five-pounds-fifty! No wonder Tony and Michelle drive a Mercedes!"

Tony and Michelle owned the hotel and the boat mooring I rented, and they'd already asked me to keep Mabel under control when she'd stolen a piece of chicken from one of the customers. I didn't think they'd take kindly to Boris spitting at their patrons. "You need to control yourself, Boris," I said.

Boris led the way across the grass as we emerged from the trees. "I'm sorry," he said. "Gladys has been rationing my brandy. She thinks I drink too much. It's making me feel a little on edge. The smell of the drinks in the beer garden got my dander up. I shall be fine within a minute or two, when you two girls give me a glass of—"

Boris's demand was interrupted by a woman's scream which made my blood run cold. There's more than one type of scream. There's the type of scream a person afraid of spiders makes when they walk into a cobweb, and there's the type of scream that chills the human soul. The scream which resonated across the canal, and made us all stop in our tracks, was the latter. The sky above the fields on the opposite bank of the canal grew dark with crows for the second time that day, and an invisible finger traced a cold line down my spine.

"Help me!" begged the desperate voice. "Somebody's killed him!"

The towpath on the side on the canal I lived on was long overgrown and forgotten, but with Boris leading the way, we tore a path through the briars and shoulder height grass, and scrambled up the crumbling embankment onto the stone bridge which carried the road to Bentbridge across the canal.

Boris pushed through a hedge, and Willow and I climbed over a gate into the field above which the cawing crows circled as the woman continued to scream.

"Over there!" said Boris, already running.

The wheat was still only knee high, and a scarecrow rose from the crops in the centre of the field. At the base of its pole was the hunched shape of the woman, her screams doing a far better job than any scarecrow ever could of preventing the crows in the sky from landing.

"He's dead!" the woman shouted as we neared her. "Someone's killed my Gerald!"

Boris came to a stuttering halt next to her, and turned away from the sight that transformed the field from a quintessential English landscape, into a blood splattered scene of gore.

Gerald Timkins lay dead in the shadow of the

scarecrow, and a ragged hole the size of a teacup saucer lay bare the contents of his abdomen. Blood seeped into the soil around his body, and vivid splashes of crimson coated the broken stalks of golden wheat which cradled him. Gerald's shotgun lay abandoned a few feet away from his body, and snapped stems of corn indicated trampled pathways through the crops in more than one direction.

Boris made a strangled cough, and Willow placed a hand on the shaking shoulder of Gerald's wife. "What happened?" she managed, her face white and her hand trembling.

I dialled the police and pressed the phone tight to my ear as Mrs Timkins sobbed her reply. "I don't know," she gasped. "Who would do this to him? He was so happy — he'd just bought some new electronic crow scarers and he only came here to take that old thing down," she said, pointing at the straw stuffed scarecrow that gazed indifferently at the macabre scene below it. "He said it was attracting the crows and not scaring them away. I got worried when he didn't come home for lunch and didn't answer his phone. I found him like this — my beautiful husband. Why would anyone want to kill my Gerald? I don't understand."

I stepped away from the murder scene as I reported the crime to the police, and pocketed my phone when I'd ended the call. "The police are on their way," I said. "I'm so sorry, Mrs Timkins."

Her body shook as she collapsed next to her husband, and her harrowing wails of anguish scared even the most determined of crows from the sky above us.

WITH THE POLICE on the scene, and statements taken from Willow and I, we made our way back to my boat, promising Barney that we were okay. The police had taken note of the time we'd seen Gerald with his shotgun near the canal, and according to Gerald's wife, we were the last people to have seen him alive — apart from his murderer of course.

We hadn't needed to remind Boris not to speak in the company of the police — he was unusually lost for words, and if a goat's face could be described as shocked — Boris looked downright anguished. He'd not uttered a single syllable on the slow walk back to the boat, and I was glad when Granny telephoned me, demanding to speak to the upset goat.

Boris spoke into my phone, which I'd placed on the dinette table next to the bottle of brandy and coffee cups. "Gladys?" he said. "Something terrible has happened."

"You're telling me!" said Granny, her voice edged

with anger. "I've never been so embarrassed in my whole life!"

Boris sighed. "There's been a murder, Gladys. An awful, awful murder."

Granny hardly paused. "I can beat that! Your credit card expired yesterday, Boris. I can't pay off the remaining balance for the Range Rover. You'd better sort this out. I want that car. It's beautiful... you should see it... black, shiny, and with leather seats which smell like a fatted calf. It's perfect, and I want it!"

Boris licked at his bowl of brandy. "Didn't you hear me?" he said. "There's been a murder. Gerald Timkins is dead. Shot. With his own gun, and with only a tatty old scarecrow present to witness his violent demise."

Granny's voice took on a no-nonsense edge. "I heard you loud and clear, but did you hear me? Your credit card has expired. There's nothing I can do for a dead man, but I'm standing here in a car showroom which smells like posh candles and fifty-pound notes, looking at a car which I can't pay for. What are you going to do about it?"

Boris snorted and rolled his eyes. "I'll phone my bank and have a new card delivered. It will be sent to my own home though. You'll have to go and collect it for me."

Granny sighed, and said something under her

breath. "Make it so, Boris. You telephone the bank right away when I end this call. Oh, and I am sorry about Gerald. He was a good farmer, not like Farmer Bill, who likes to throw around unfounded accusations of sexual assault. I think it's to do with what they farm, to be frank. It's a far more peaceful farmer who grows plants, than one who raises livestock to be slaughtered or milked. I shall visit Mrs Timkins at the earliest opportunity and offer her my condolences."

The sexual assault accusations from Farmer Bill stemmed back to an incident in the Coffee Pot Café. Granny had been adamant she'd been reaching into Farmer Bill's crotch area to retrieve an item of dropped food. Framer Bill said differently, and had embarrassed Granny in front of the other diners. Grammy had never lived down the humiliation.

Granny ended the call with a final reminder that we should still be at my mother's for the meal at seven o'clock, whether a murder had occurred or not, and Boris did as he had promised, telephoning his bank under the guise of Charleston and arranging for a new card to be express delivered the next day.

Susie arrived at the boat at six o'clock and took over guardianship of Boris, and Willow and I got showered, changed, and left the two of them to drink brandy and elderberry wine as they watched *Robot Wars* on the television which Willow had insisted I installed when she'd moved aboard.

A tight ball of tension grew in my stomach as Willow and I headed to mum's cottage. Already that day I'd seen a fat man losing the plot over celery, a candlelit vigil involving a goat, a policeman under the influence of a magic spell, and a dead body.

I took a deep breath and relaxed a little. We were on our way to a civilised family meal, and I very much doubted anything else could go wrong on that day.

That would have just been unfair.

CHAPTER SEVEN

We arrived at Hazelwood cottage with fifteen minutes to spare. Granny had arrived before us, in a taxi, and she took Willow and I aside when we arrived, making us promise we'd take her to Charleston's house the next day to pick up the new credit card.

It was nice to be back at the cottage I'd grown up in, and Willow and I took a short walk around the private woodland which surrounded Mum's home, shaking the gory memories of Gerald Timkins's dead body from our minds before we sat down for a family meal.

It seemed odd to be crowded around a table with my family as a woman on the other side of Wickford mourned the murder of her husband, but Granny had put things in perspective as she'd helped Mum lay the big table. "Life goes on," she'd said, "and we'd all do well to celebrate the living as well as the dead. You never know when a tragedy will strike, so cherish those around you while you still can."

Barney had managed to arrive by seven o'clock as Granny had instructed, and had refused to give Willow any information when she'd asked him about Gerald's murder. "Not tonight, Willow" he said, with an apologetic smile. "The detectives are investigating, but it's early days yet. I'd like to forget about what I saw in that field today and enjoy this meal."

"Nobody's enjoying any meal until that brother of mine gets here," said Mum, diverting the conversation from the subject of murder. "Trust him to be late to his own welcome meal!"

"He'll be here soon enough," said Granny. "Brian would never miss free food without a bloody good reason. He's probably got stuck in traffic."

Barney sat to my right, and I gasped as his hand tightened on my bare thigh beneath the table. There were better ways for a man to let a woman know he was interested in her than groping her at a family meal, and I lifted my hand in readiness to deliver the slap which would indicate to Barney Dobkins that he'd chosen the wrong method to woo me. My hand faltered inches from Barney's face as his mouth opened and he made a sound which attracted the attention of everyone around the table.

"What's wrong, Barney?" I said, worried the gargling in his throat and the tightening grip of his fingers on my leg were symptoms of some sort of seizure, maybe induced by the trauma of what he'd witnessed in the field earlier that day.

"Oh no," said Willow. "Oh no!"

Granny and Mum both turned to look over their shoulders as Barney pointed a trembling finger at the lounge doorway. The deep humming sound that filled the room told me precisely what was happening before I dared to look for myself. A portal to the haven was opening, but as everybody in the room with magical powers was seated safely at the table, it could only mean one thing — it was an incoming portal, and judging by the colour of the light that filled the doorway, there could only be one person who had activated it. Uncle Brian.

The colour of a haven portal was said to reflect the personality of the person who'd conjured it, and the vivid lilac glow that bathed the kitchen in bright light, was certainly a reflection of my uncle's personality.

The doorway quivered and creaked, and the light grew brighter as the throbbing hum grew louder. Barney did his best impression of a fish out of water, and his fingers hurt my thigh as they dug deep into muscle. His other hand shook as he pointed at the doorway, and a sliver of drool hung from his bottom lip. Poor Barney. He'd already been victim to a magic spell earlier in the day, seen a dead body, and was about to meet my Uncle Brian. How much more could one mortal take in one day?

Two matching green suitcases appeared from the shimmering pool of light, and the disembodied voice of my uncle echoed around the kitchen, throbbing in perfect harmony with the spell. "Only me-ee! Anybody home?"

His belly emerged before the rest of his body, and Barney released my thigh from his grip as he stood up slowly and picked up a steak knife from the table, holding it in front of him as Brian's grinning face emerged.

"Who's the ginger ninja with the knife?" said Brian, dropping his cases and removing his hat. "He could do somebody an injury. Oooh, you've got your best china on the table, Maggie!"

"Brian!" said Granny, standing and taking the bright blue Trilby from her son's outstretched hand. "My first born! How are you, my sweet angel?"

Brian wrapped Granny in his arms, and Barney waved the knife in erratic circles as Granny led her son towards the empty seat at the head of the table.

"What are you doing, Brian?" said Mum, taking her brother's herringbone tweed jacket from him, and tossing it onto the rocking chair in the corner, next to the fireplace. "You said you were coming by car! You know how dangerous it is to attempt a reverse portal, you could have ended up anywhere!"

That was true. It was brave witch indeed who conjured up a portal from the haven to a place they hadn't entered the magical dimension from. Witches could utilise any entrance in our world to use as an anchor point for a portal into the haven, but it was standard, and safe, practice to use the same portal you'd arrived through as an exit point. Conjuring a portal to a place you hadn't arrived from was tempting fate — a witch could end up anywhere if they couldn't *perfectly* picture the place they wanted to arrive at in their mind's eye. One witch had caused widespread panic, and a half-day for the staff at a hardware store, when her portal had inadvertently opened in a display door as a salesman pointed out the finer points of the brass fittings to a young couple hoping to upgrade their new home.

"I didn't fancy driving," explained Brian, "and anyway, I've stood in this kitchen enough times to know I can safely open a portal in it."

"Erm…" I said, laying a reassuring hand on Barney's arm. "There's more to worry about than how Uncle Brian got here." I jerked my thumb at Barney. "What about him?"

Brian leaned across the table and took the knife from Barney's shaking hand. "Doesn't he know we're witches?" he said with a smile. "How exciting! It's been a long time since I've seen that look on some-body's face! Look, he's terrified." He softened his tone. "Don't be scared," he said, "we don't bite... unless you want us to!"

Granny giggled and Barney gurgled.

"Oh, Brian!" said Granny. "It's so good to have you home. It's about time we had somebody with a sense of humour around here again. How are you, my beautiful strapping boy?"

I jerked my thumb at Barney again, who'd begun sweating. "Erm... what about Barney? He looks very peaky."

"Never mind him," said Mum, "we'll sort him out in a moment. One of us will cast a spell on him, and he'll be convinced Brian arrived by taxi — as he should have if he was too lazy to drive."

Brian sat down and stuffed a napkin into the collar of his perfectly pressed shirt. "I'm not lazy — I'm hungry," he declared. "I haven't eaten since four."

"Forget your stomach, uncle Brian," I said, begin-ning to anger. "There's a man standing next to me in fear for his life. Will somebody please help him?"

Willow stood up and raised her hand. "I'll do it," she said. "I'll use the same spell I used on him this morning."

Barney turned his head slowly and stared at me with pleading eyes. "What's going on, Penny?" he said.

"Sit down, Willow," said Granny, pushing her seat alongside Brian's and placing an empty glass in front of him. "You can't use the same spell on him twice in the same day. You'll fry his wiring. Maggie, you do it, I'm sure Penelope doesn't want to hex her beau." She tapped Brian's empty glass with a long fingernail. "Somebody fetch me a bottle of *Wickford Head-banger*. My little man looks thirsty."

Wickford Headbanger was the town brewery's most infamous and strongest beer. It had won awards all over Britain and was rumoured to be a cure for bunions and an elixir for dying plants. I'd once poured a little into one of my mother's dried out and neglected basil plants, but rather than bringing it back to full health, the plant had immediately wilted into total oblivion. My mother was sure the sound we'd heard had been the wind blowing under the kitchen door, but I was convinced it had been a botanical sigh of acceptance as the plant had finally been able to give up its battle with life.

"That would be splendid," said Brian. "Fetch that tall ginger chap one too. He looks like his whistle needs wetting."

Brian's plump red face widened into a toothy grin, and sparks of rage blossomed in the deepest pit of my stomach. I gritted my teeth and stared at my uncle through eyes which twitched with anger. "His name is

Barney," I hissed, "and he deserves your respect, not your ridicule. Can't you see how scared he is?"

Barney slumped into his seat and stared up at me. "Who are you, Penny?" he said. "And why is that fat impeccably dressed man making fun of me?"

"Have a drink, Barney," I said. "You're in shock." I looked around the table. "Okay," I said. "It's obviously only me and Willow who care about how Barney's feeling. You three don't seem to give a damn that Barney's witnessing a dysfunctional witch family having dinner, so I've made a decision. I'm telling Barney all about us, and no-one is going to cast a spell on him to make him forget. He deserves to know the truth after what he's been through today."

Granny tittered under her breath and poured Brian's beer into his glass. "You enjoy good head, don't you, son?" she said as froth rose up the walls of the glass.

"I love *a* good head, Mother! A good head *on* my beer! Good grief, sometimes I wonder if you know what you're saying."

Granny smiled. "Maggie, cast a spell on young PC Dobkins would you. Penelope's right, he shouldn't be witnessing this."

Mum waved an idle hand in front of her, and blue sparks danced at her fingertips.

Barney made a squeak like a balloon vomiting air,

and I placed a hand on his shoulder. "Don't worry," I said. "You'll be okay. Nobody's going to hurt you."

Mum pressed her finger and thumb together, but before she could click them and cast her spell, a swell of rising energy rushed through my body which exited my body through the fingertips of both hands. "I said no spells!" I shouted, crockery and cutlery shaking on the tabletop as magic streamed from me and counteracted Mum's spell with a loud cracking sound which made her shriek.

Mum shook her hand in the air as if she'd been burnt, and her sparks fizzled out. Granny stood up, and Brian gazed at me with a nervous respect. My sister placed her hand in mine as I stumbled backwards, and Barney finally let out his fear in a scream which hurt my ears.

"Where on earth did you learn that?" said Granny. "That was real magic right there!"

"I don't know," I said, my eyes sliding closed with the sort of heavy sleepiness I hadn't experienced since I'd had my first alcoholic drink. What I did know, though, as I gave myself to sleep, was that I knew how to open a portal in a doorway.

I'd been given my entry spell to the haven.

CHAPTER EIGHT

I woke to the gentle touch of Susie's hand on mine and the rancid stench of Boris's brandy breath burning my nostrils. Rosie licked my arm and I tickled her behind the ear.

"What happened?" I said, squeezing Susie's fingers and pushing Boris away from my face with my free hand. I recognised the low white ceiling above me and the softness of the mattress below me. The picture of Granny, Mum and Willow on the wall to my right confirmed it. I was on my boat, in my bedroom. The unmistakeable sound of the bird dawn chorus outside told me I'd been asleep for a while. "How did I get here?" I asked, propping myself up on an elbow. I was certain I hadn't so much as tasted a *Wickford Headbanger* at the meal, and the headache I had was not a hangover. "I remember what happened at the dinner table, but then everything's a blank."

"You passed out," said Susie, moving aside as I swung my legs out of bed. "After you cast your spell. Willow said she'd never seen anything like it, and Barney was worried sick about you. He carried you onto the boat and wanted to stay with you until you woke up, but he had to go to work early this morning. The police are searching the field that Gerald was murdered in for clues."

"Where's Willow?" I said, the smell of bacon being fried giving me a clue.

"Making breakfast," said Boris, "she was very worried about you so we gave her something to do, although I'm beginning to regret it. She tried to *grill* my bacon. She said it was more healthy, or some such hippy nonsense. I had quite the argument with her, didn't I, Susie?"

Susie sighed. "Yes, Boris, you did, and the language you used made Barney blush."

I stared at Boris. "You spoke in front of Barney?" I said. "So he still knows we're witches? Mum didn't cast a spell on him to make him forget when I passed out?"

Susie passed me my dressing gown, and I slipped it over my thigh length sleeping shirt. I hoped it had been Susie or Willow who had undressed me, and not Barney, or goddess forbid, Boris. I was sure his hooves couldn't have undone the laces on my boots, but I wasn't convinced he couldn't have pulled my dress over my head.

"Barney knows everything," said Susie. "Willow stopped anyone from casting a spell on him and he's taking the whole thing remarkably well. Apart from when Boris first spoke to him of course. He was okay after a glass of brandy though."

"I've never seen such a tall man fall over," said Boris. "It was quite spectacular. Quite beautiful, really — he reminded me of a marionette at the ends of a master puppeteer's strings."

Willow appeared in the doorway to my bedroom, her hair tied in a loose bun, and the apron she wore splattered with the evidence of greasy cooking. "You're awake!" she said, looking me up and down and taking me in her arms. "Are you alright?"

"I'm fine," I said. "Really."

"What happened?" said my sister. "How did you cast that spell? Mum and Granny said it was very advanced pure magic, and Uncle Brian said it was better than the Yorkshire puddings Mum had cooked."

My memory was muddled. I could only recall the anger bubbling in my stomach as Barney sat next to me staring at me in fear, and the surge of power through my arms as I'd cast the spell. My mind began putting the pieces together and I caught my breath as the last thing I remembered came flooding back. "I know how to get to the haven," I said, the hairs on the back of my neck standing rigid. "I have my entry spell."

Willow shrieked and Susie clasped her hands together.

Boris snorted. "That's all well and good," he said, "but there's more important things to consider. I can smell black pudding burning."

"Do it," said Willow, pointing at the door which led onto the stern decking. "Make your portal!"

Susie agreed. "You have to! This is so exciting!"

"Black pudding emergency," said Boris, tapping Willow's leg with a hoof.

Willow rushed out of the bedroom to deal with the cooking dilemma, and I took a deep breath. I was sure there had to be more to it than just casting my spell and expecting a portal to open, but I'd seen Mum and Granny do it hundreds of times. Maybe it was that simple.

"Shouldn't I wait?" I said as Willow hurried back into the room, squeezing past Boris and standing next to me at the foot of the two steps that led from my bedroom onto the boat deck. "There's a ritual, isn't there? Mum will come through with me and Aunt Eva will want to meet me on the other side."

"That's only for the first time you go through it," said Willow. "You can open it and see what colour it is, nobody will mind that!"

Susie smiled. "Go on," she said. "Open it already!"

"If it means I'll get my breakfast any quicker, I wholeheartedly agree," said Boris. "Just open the damn thing before the sausages go cold! They're pork and leek, Susie picked them up from the butcher's for me yesterday. It's an old family recipe, apparently. The leeks are Welsh and the pork is — " The doorway creaking and quivering cut Boris short. "Wow," he muttered.

"It's beautiful," said Willow, "and it matches your personality perfectly."

A soft breeze blew across my face as I took a step closer to the inviting golden glow that filled the doorway. It had been easy to open, far easier than I'd ever imagined — almost an anti-climax after waiting for my spell for so long.

Willow took my hand in hers. "Congratulations, Penelope Weaver," she whispered, her voice hardly audible above the gentle hum of the spell. "You're a real witch now."

I closed my eyes and allowed the portal to close. The temptation to walk through it was too great, but I knew it would devastate Mum if she couldn't open her own portal and enter the haven with me on my first trip. "I am, aren't I?" I said. I squeezed her hand tight. "It'll be your turn soon, Willow."

WITH BREAKFAST EATEN and Boris's beard cleaned of the food detritus that clung to it, Willow and I prepared to take Boris home and pick Granny up for our trip to collect the credit card.

Susie had left to begin the job of reporting on Gerald's murder. The police were holding a press conference at ten o'clock, and Barney had promised her a front row seat.

Willow had explained why nobody had cast a spell on Barney after I'd fainted. "They wanted to," she said, "but I talked them out of it. Barney promised he wouldn't say a word to anyone, and Granny made him swear on his police badge. Uncle Brian was happy with a pinky promise."

"What about Mum?" I said.

"She was more concerned with finding out if Barney thought the prawn cocktail starter would have been nicer with some melba toast, and checking whether you'd hurt yourself when you fell over."

I put a hand to the back of my head and felt for lumps. "And?" I said.

"He said he wasn't too fussed on any toast, Melba or not. He was in shock though. He could hardly speak."

I laughed. "I meant was I injured at all!"

"Oh! Just a small bruise on your chin. Uncle

Brian healed it, but he put on a bit of a show for Barney's benefit. You know how he is."

I nodded. Uncle Brian had always reminded me of the swanky magicians that made their money on TV shows. His three year infatuation with crushed velvet jackets had reinforced that image of him beyond any redemption.

"He draped his polka dot hanky over your face and asked me to be his assistant. I had to swipe the hanky away when he'd waved his hand over you. Barney clapped, but I think he was still in fear for his life at that stage. It was polite applause more than genuine admiration. You were fine though, Uncle Brian gave you a full medical inspection and declared you were in a temporary magical sleep. Mum insisted Barney finished his dinner before she let us take you back to the boat. She told me that the spotted dick she made for pudding would seal the deal on Barney keeping his mouth shut about us. It *was* quite nice, I have to admit. Barney had two helpings."

Fourteen missed calls from Barney were displayed on my phone, and I messaged him to tell him I'd speak to him that evening and answer all his questions. I was sure he'd have a lot of them, and I proposed that we go to the little Italian place on the outskirts of town for a meal. Barney accepted with a text that finished with three kisses, and I sent him one of my own in return. The previous night's events had proved to me that my feelings for Barney couldn't be ignored anymore. I'd experienced a protectiveness for him that had ran deep in my veins, and I wasn't one to ignore my emotions. There was a reason I cared for him, and I wanted to explore it.

It seemed that the previous night had been more than just a catalyst for a new era in my magical life. It had helped move my personal life forward too, and as Willow, Boris, and I, climbed the footpath to the hotel carpark, I allowed the butterflies in my stomach to soar as high as they liked.

It was a good day, and I deserved a good day.

CHAPTER NINE

*G*ranny sat in the passenger seat and Willow sat in the back of the Renault, rubbing white goat hairs from her black leggings. The neighbourhood Boris had give us directions to was in the the most upmarket area of Covenhill. Every tree that lined the pavement was perfectly trimmed and manicured, and it had been at least a mile since I'd seen any rubbish in the gutters.

"Are you sure Boris likes living in your cottage, Granny?" joked Willow. "It looks like he was used to a little more luxury in his life before he met you."

Granny peered between the gap in the two front seats. "Boris is happy where he is," she said, "and if he wasn't, he'd have wanted to come with us today, wouldn't he? Anyway, he'll have all the luxury he desires when I can finally pay for the Range Rover."

"Don't take advantage of him," I warned. "He may have money, but at the end of the day he's trapped in the body of a goat. His decisions might not be good ones."

Granny turned slowly to face me as I took a left turn into Gladiola Drive. "How dare you!" she said. "*How dare you*! Me take advantage of somebody? I've spent my whole life fighting against the injustices of society. I should be applauded for what I've done *for* the disadvantaged, not accused of *taking* advantage of somebody." She shook her head woefully. "I don't know, Penelope. Ever since you got your spell for the haven you've been a different person. A very different person indeed! You've changed. Don't let it go to your head, young lady. Every witch gets their spell eventually — you're not a special case. Bring yourself back down to earth amongst us commoners would you?"

"She only got it last night, and she spent most of that time unconscious," said Willow, leaning through the gap in the seats as we approached the large house at the end of the cul-de-sac. "And we only picked you up twenty-five minutes ago, Granny. Penny has hardly had the time to change her socks, let alone make you think she's changed her whole outlook on life."

"We're here," I said, defusing the tension. Granny muttered something under her breath as I parked the car in the red-brick driveway and peered at the large house. "It's beautiful."

The large house was a modern build, but based on Georgian architecture. Built from cream stone, and with a narrow parapet at the rim of the roof, it loomed against the tall scotch pines which grew beyond it. Pillars framed the wide front door, and the garden was immaculate. "He must still be paying a gardener," I said.

"Boris is paying *all* his bills," said Granny, defensively. "Letting the credit card expire was a simple mistake on his behalf. Come on, let's get inside, pick up his card, and go home. Rich people neighbourhoods make me want to vomit blood. They're so pretentious, and they smell of envy."

"Says the woman who's only here so she can buy a prestigious car," said Willow with a giggle.

Granny chose to ignore Willow, and scampered up the driveway, looking around at the neighbouring homes with furtive glances that made her look every bit like an elderly burglar, or a shy gypsy woman trying to sell lucky heathers to the wealthy. "Around the back," said Granny, leading me and Willow around the side of the house. "Boris said the alarm won't go off if we use the back door. He forgot to set it before he came to my cottage on that fateful night."

"That disastrous night," I mumbled, standing next to Granny as she slid a key from her apron pocket and opened the tall sliding doors which looked out over the large rear garden.

The doors made a gentle whooshing sound as Granny prised them open and stepped inside Charleston Huang's home. "Wipe your feet," she ordered, scrubbing the soles of her sandals on a Persian rug.

"I don't think that's a doormat, Granny," I said. "It looks like it's worth a lot of money."

"Only a rich fool would put something worth a lot of money on the floor next to a door," said Granny. "Boris is no fool, of course it's a doormat. Now come on, don't touch anything, we just have to get to the front door, find the letter from his bank, and pick up the personal belongings he wants me to bring home. We're looking for a silver framed photograph of his parents, and a pair of antique wooden clogs. The clogs are for me, Boris said they'll stop me dragging my feet. He says they force one to lift one's feet *and* force good posture. I'm *not* to drive in them though. Boris said I could cause all manner of accidents."

I'd have loved to have been a fly on the wall at Ashwood cottage when Granny and Boris had a private conversation. How the subject of clogs had ever come up intrigued me, but I decided to help Granny find them nonetheless. "I'll look for the clogs," I said. "Willow, you find the photo, and Granny can get the card. I don't want to be in here longer than we have to. The car looks out of place in this neighbourhood — somebody might phone the police."

"He said the photograph is in the living room and the clogs are upstairs," said Granny sneaking through the kitchen, admiring the huge chrome stove as she passed it, and disappearing through the doorway.

Willow rushed off to find the photograph for Boris, and I headed up the stairs to look for Dutch footwear. Hardwood floors thumped under my boots as I navigated each of the five bedrooms looking for the clogs, and I couldn't help but admire Boris's choice of minimalistic decor. With plain off-white walls dotted with seascapes and modern art, and no clutter to be seen anywhere, it was the sort of home I'd have liked to live in if I was ever persuaded to leave my boat and live on land.

I found the clogs in the third bedroom I looked in, placed on top of a mahogany sideboard, next to a carved wooden duck and a photograph of Charleston standing on the great wall of China. He'd once told us that he'd been to visit the country of his ancestors, but had found the whole experience underwhelming. The sullen face staring back at mc from the photograph confirmed he'd been telling the truth. He looked downright miserable.

A photograph on the wall above the sideboard caught my attention. I'd seen the lady somewhere before, I knew I had, I just couldn't place her. The black and white photograph looked very old, and the lady in the picture was dressed in a ballet dancing outfit and was standing alone on a stage. I lifted the photograph from the wall and ran a finger over the old image. I'd definitely seen the woman before, and I decided to take the photograph with me so I could ask Boris about it.

Granny rifled through the stack of letters she'd placed on the small table next to the front door. "Is the credit card there?" I said, holding out the clogs for her to inspect.

She patted her apron pocket in answer to my question and gave the clogs a cursory glance, nodding her approval. "What's that?" she said, pointing at the photo I'd brought downstairs with me.

I held it up for Granny to inspect. "The woman looks familiar," I said. "I wanted to ask Boris about her."

Granny pushed her glasses closer to her eyes, and took the photo from me. "Heavens above," she said under her breath. "I knew it!"

"Knew what?" said Willow, emerging from the dining room with the silver framed photo of Boris's parents under her arm. She joined Granny in studying the Chinese ballet dancer. "Hey, I recognise that woman, Granny," she said. "She's in your old photograph album!"

Of course! That's where I'd seen her! Why did Granny and Boris both have a photograph of the same woman though? "Who is she, Granny?" I said.

"This explains everything!" said Granny. "I told you that the night Charleston came to me was fateful, didn't I, Penelope? He was brought to me by magic and fate!"

"You said you found him in the phone book, Granny," said Willow, helpfully. "Under acupuncturists. How is that fate?"

"Oh, it's fate alright!" beamed Granny. "There's no such thing as a coincidence. This photo explains so much, girls! The woman you're looking at was a witch. Her name was Chang-Chang, and I know she had secrets. She's one of the very few witches who chose to die in this world. She visited the haven on occasion, but when her time came, she remained in this world instead of choosing immortality in the haven. I'll bet my bottom dollar that the woman in this photograph is Charleston's grandmother, and that would mean that Charleston has magic! If that's not fate, I don't know what is!"

"Why didn't Boris tell you?" said Willow. "Surely he would know something?"

"Who knows?" said Granny. "Maybe he knew, maybe he didn't. But it's fate that brought him to my house that night, and it's fate that sent Penelope up those stairs looking for clogs, and coming down those stairs with this photograph!"

"And the clogs," I reminded her.

"Yes. Yes," said Granny. "And the clogs. Come on, girls, let's get out of here! There's lots to do! First you need to take me to Mrs Timkins's farm so I can offer her my condolences, and then you can take me to the Range Rover dealership so I can pick up my new car!"

"And then you can ask Boris about this photograph?" I said.

"I'll leave that for a day tor two," said Granny. "I'll need to work out how to ask him. It is very personal after all, and you know me... I like to be tactful."

CHAPTER TEN

*T*wo sheepdogs ran to greet us as I parked the Renault outside Gerald Timkins's home. The large house was at the end of a long bumpy track, and the field that Gerald had died in was hidden in the valley below us. The dogs acted as if nothing was out of the ordinary, but the drawn curtains in the windows of the old farmhouse told a different story.

Willow stroked one of the sheepdogs, and Granny shooed another away as she clambered from the car. "When my Norman died, rest his soul, Sandra Timkins came to visit me. Now the shoe's firmly on the other foot. The circle is complete."

"Granny!" snapped Willow. "Do you know how awful that sounded?"

"Nonsense," said Granny. "That's just how it is.

Come on, the front door's wide open, Sandra's probably out in the fields, sowing seeds or pulling up lovely fat turnips, or whatever it is that farmer's wives do — baking a cake, I don't know. What I mean is she's probably too busy to let yesterday's tragic murder of her husband get her down."

Granny stomped straight into the house without knocking on the open door, the dogs alongside her. "Coooee!" she yelled. "It's only me, Gladys Weaver, come to offer my condolences! My granddaughters are with me too! We've come in their car, I'm off to pick up a brand new Range Rover when I leave here. Perhaps I should have come to see you *after* I'd collected the new vehicle — it would have dealt with the farm-track a lot better than that shitty little Renault did! Sandra? Are you here?"

Willow and I followed her into the house with a lot more dignity, wiping our feet on the thick doormat as we stepped inside the gloomy hallway. The smell of baking bread hung in the air, and music was being played somewhere in the farmhouse. Maybe Granny had been right. Maybe farmer's wives *were* too busy to spend all of their time mourning when a loved one had passed over.

"Sandra!" shouted Granny. "Where are you?"

"I'm in here," came Sandra's voice. "In the living room. Doing the ironing."

"Told you," said Granny over her shoulder. "Getting on with things. It's the best way."

We followed Granny through the crooked doorway into the living room. It seemed Sandra wasn't coping as well as Granny had imagined. She sat on the sofa, next to a pile of clothes, with an item of clothing clasped in her hands. She brought it to her face and sniffed it, her body shaking as she sobbed. "I'm sorry," she said. "I was doing the ironing, and I could still smell Gerald on this t-shirt," she said. "It's very hard to accept that he won't be wearing it again." Sandra took another long smell of the shirt, and placed it next to her on the sofa. "Sit down, please," she said. "I'll make you all a cup of tea."

"Are you on your own?" said Willow. "How are you coping?"

Sandra sniffed, and dabbed her eyes with a tissue she took from the beneath the sleeve of her jumper. "The police liaison officer wanted to stay with me," she said, "but I sent her away. I'll do better on my own. Gerald's sister is coming tomorrow, she *was* coming to spend a week with her big brother, but now she's going to be helping me arrange his funeral!"

"Oh, Sandra," said Granny, sitting next to the distraught woman and placing her hand on her shoulder. "I'm so sorry. Have the police got any idea who killed him yet?"

"Granny," I said. "Perhaps Sandra doesn't want to talk about things like that."

Sandra smiled at me. "It's okay," she said. "And I hope you two girls are alright, too. It couldn't have been easy for you both to see my husband like that. I was very thankful that you waited with me until the police arrived."

"It was the least we could do," said Willow, looking at the floor. She lifted her eyes. "Let us know if there's anything else we can do to help."

"Thank you," Sandra said, "I know I'll cope. I *have* to. That's what Gerald would have wanted, but I'm not going to pretend it'll be easy. Finding out who killed my husband will help, of course, but things will never be the same without Gerald. We've been together for forty years. Since we met in school."

"Do the police know anything *at all*?" said Granny. "Have they got a suspect yet?"

If Granny was speaking out of turn it didn't seem to bother Sandra. She dabbed at her eyes with the tissue. "Only the people he'd argued with recently," she said. "Gerald wasn't really the type of man to make enemies, though. He just had misunderstandings with folk."

"Who had he argued with?" said Granny, perching on the edge of the sofa and taking Sandra's hand in hers. "Farmer Bill, by any chance? Don't you think he's got cold eyes, Sandra? Violent eyes, one might say. The empty eyes of an unkind man, almost."

"Granny!" I said. Now was *not* the time to be bringing up her vendetta against Farmer Bill. "Why don't you make the tea? I'm sure Sandra would like a cup."

"That would be lovely, Gladys," agreed Sandra. "If you don't mind, of course. You could take the bread out of the oven for me too? It's been in for ten minutes too long already."

"I *suppose* I could," said Granny, a little reluctantly. "You two can update me when I come back," she said, looking at me and Willow.

I nodded and Willow shrugged. Granny made her way into the kitchen and found the source of the music, switching it off.

"The police don't really have anything to go on, yet," said Sandra, ignoring Granny's outburst about farmer Bill. Most people in Wickford knew Granny, and most people in Wickford knew how to ignore her too. "It's early days. They want to speak to that horrible birdwatching woman… Mrs Oliver," she said. "She doesn't understand the damage that crows can do to a crop, they need to be kept under control, and the scarecrows weren't working. He *had* to shoot at those birds, and that woman wouldn't leave him alone, always shouting at him and running to the police. I doubt she shot Gerald though. She's all bark and no bite."

Sandra picked the T-shirt up and took another smell.

"Had he argued with anybody else?" said Willow.

"Just the buyers for his crops, but that was always happening. That's part of the farming business though, isn't it? And they weren't really arguments… more like negotiations really. Gerald didn't really argue with people, he just got on with life, and let others get on with theirs. He was a good, kind man."

"Tea's up!" said Granny, storming back into the room with a tray balanced in front of her. "Your bread's ruined though, Sandra. It might be alright toasted with a little marmite on it to disguise its inferiority, but I'd not want a cheese sandwich made from it, thank you very much! It looks and smells *vile*."

I hoped I'd never turn out like Granny when I was her age. Watching Granny negotiate normal life was like watching a trained chimp riding a bike — it went through the motions, without knowing why, and without caring what happened around it.

"Never-mind," said Sandra, moving the T-shirt aside so Granny could sit down. "I'll bake another loaf. It will give me something productive to do."

Sandra laid the T-shirt out over the arm of the sofa and took a cup from Granny. "Thank you. Gladys," she said. "I do appreciate you coming to see me."

"Sandra," I said, my gaze still on the t-shirt. "Your husband was the tank?"

Printed on the red t-shirt in a large white font was the simple sentence — *The Tank - Pie-eating champion of South England.*

Sandra smiled. "Yes," she said, with a gentle pride in her voice. "Gerald was unbeatable for years. He retired after winning for three years consecutively — it was a record! Nobody had won for three years in a row before. He retired because he was getting a little podgy from all the practice! I was forever having to let his trousers out and put new holes in his belt." Sandra's eyes twinkled as she remembered. "He only came out of retirement because somebody's getting close to beating his record of three consecutive wins. He just couldn't accept it. That was Gerald for you, though — very competitive!"

"Had he argued with anyone about the pie-eating contest?" I said, glancing at Willow. "Another competitor perhaps?"

Sandra shook her head. "Of course not. It's just friendly rivalry between them." She picked the T-shirt up and held it close to her chest. "Why are you asking these questions?" she said. "Do you know something? Do you know who killed my Gerald?"

Granny looked at me with a raised eyebrow. "Well? Do you? And why am I only just finding out about this? Does gossip not get passed up the chain of command in our family anymore?"

I gave Willow another look. "A man came into the shop, yesterday. He mentioned the tank coming out of retirement and he wasn't happy… was he, Willow?"

"No," said Willow. "He said some quite nasty things about your husband, Sandra, but he didn't use Gerald's real name, or we'd have told the police by now. We didn't know Gerald was the tank, you see."

Sandra stood up and grabbed her phone. "Do you know the man's name?" she said, already dialling the police.

"Felix Round," I said.

CHAPTER ELEVEN

*W*illow and I dropped Granny off at the Range Rover dealership and headed back to the boat, with the intention of transferring the shop stock from the *Water Witch* to its new home in town.

The police had come quickly to Sandra's house and taken our statements regarding Felix Round and his outburst in the shop. Luckily for me, Barney wasn't one of the police officers who was sent. I was nervous about seeing him. It wasn't everyday that a mortal found out you were a witch, especially a mortal for whom you had feelings. I'd answer all his questions of course, but I was beginning to wonder if I'd done the right thing. Maybe I should have let somebody cast a spell on him at the dinner table.

Maybe it would have been easier all round for everybody concerned.

After hearing our stories, the police were eager to speak to Felix Round, and had begun looking for him in town. It made me shudder to think the man who'd stood a foot away from me the day before could have been a murderer.

Mabel ran to greet us as we crossed the grass towards the boat, and Rosie watched us from her vantage point on the roof, sitting next to the tin chimney, licking a paw and swishing her tail.

Willow heard the music before me. "Someone's on the boat!" she said.

"It must be Susie," I said. "I gave her a spare key for the boat and the new shop, and she gave me one for her flat. Maybe she's got news from the press conference."

"That's not Susie," said Willow, as a baritone singing voice flooded from the open bow doors. "That's Uncle Brian!"

As Elton John hit the chorus of *Rocket Man*, Uncle Brian raised his game too, causing Mabel to let out a warbling howl, and making Rosie jump.

"He's found the music channel on the TV," I said, climbing aboard the boat and down into the little room which was still a magic shop, but would very soon be Willow's bedroom.

The aroma of freshly brewed coffee filled the

boat, and I could detect the scent of men's aftershave too.

Uncle Brian sat in the built-in dinette area which folded down into the bed which Willow had slept on since she'd moved aboard. The coffee percolator was bubbling away on one of the kitchen counters, and Uncle Brian was singing between mouthfuls of the sandwich he was eating. A newspaper was spread out in front of him, and he gave us a wide grin when he saw us.

"My favourite nieces!" he said, grabbing the TV remote control and lowering the volume. "How are you both today? It was quite the night last night, wasn't it? I hope Barney's alright now. He had quite the scare!"

"Barney's fine," said Willow, "but what are you doing here, Uncle Brian?"

Uncle Brian took another bite of his sandwich. "I came to see if you needed help moving your shop," he said, crumbs spilling from his mouth and onto the dating advert page of the newspaper. "Maggie told me all about your new shop premises in town, and I wanted to help. She said you'd be starting work on it today. It's been a long time since I've been able to do anything for you two."

"And how did you get in?" I asked. "The doors were all locked."

Uncle Brian put his hand in the air and wiggled

his fingers. "Nothing's out of bounds to Brian Weaver's magical fingers!" he laughed. "I magicked my way in of course. I hope you don't mind? I waited on the picnic bench for you to come home, but that goose of yours wouldn't leave me alone. It was the last straw when it started humping my leg. I had to get away from it."

"Of course we don't mind," I said. "You're family, Uncle Brian, and Willow told me what you did for me last night — healing the bruise on my chin when I passed out. Thank you."

Uncle Brian smiled. "You are *more* than welcome! I'm that sort of chap, you see... a caring fellow. I've only ever used my magic for good, unlike my mother and sister, and I hope you girls will follow in my footsteps and not theirs. Talking of magic, Penny, when are you going to take your first steps into the haven? We're all very excited about it, you know? Especially me! There's nothing like seeing a witch entering the haven for the first time! It makes me tingle just to think about it!"

"I'm going to ask Mum," I said, sitting down next to Uncle Brian. "She'll want to come with me on my first trip. To show me around I suppose."

Uncle Brian put his hand on mine. "Haven't you been tempted yet? When I got my spell I was through my portal faster than a fat kid does through candy, and I can tell you from experience that a fat kid goes

103

through candy *extremely* quickly," he said, laying a hand on his belly.

Both he and my mother had been overweight kids, and neither of them had managed to lose their puppy fat, despite Granny attempting to help them both lose weight by casting numerous spells on them over the years. Some of the spells had seemed spiteful rather than helpful, especially the one that had made my mum dislike cake on her own birthday.

"Of course I'm tempted," I said, "I even opened my portal to see what colour it would be, but I didn't go through it. I want Mum to be with me."

"You opened it!" said Uncle Brian."What colour was it? No! Let me guess!" He placed a hand on my head and closed his eyes for a few seconds. "I think it was red. I saw you stick up for Barney last night, you showed real courage, and you have a powerful aura about you, Penelope. I bet it was red! That has to be your colour! It was, wasn't it?"

I shook my head. "It was gold," I said with a grin.

"It was *really* gold," agreed Willow. "Like looking inside a pirate's treasure chest!"

Uncle Brian nodded and smiled. "Gold is good. It shows you have integrity, Penelope. It's an honest colour."

Willow took Uncle Brian's empty plate from in front of him, and put it in the kitchen sink ready to be washed. She rubbed her hands together and grinned.

"Right. Are we going to get this shop moved, or sit around chatting all day? I can't wait to have my own bedroom!"

Uncle Brian stood up and straightened the folded handkerchief in the breast pocket of his pinstripe jacket. "I'm ready," he said. "I won't help with the heavy stuff of course, but I can certainly carry some paperwork or light herbs. I'm better suited at helping you work out how your new shop will look." He paused for a moment. "On second thoughts, ladies — I'll be in charge of setting up the new shop, and you girls can do all the carrying. How's that sound to you both? Fair?"

I winked at my sister. "It sounds fair to me," I smiled. I handed my uncle the key for the shop. "Why don't you head up the footpath and let yourself in, you can start planning where everything should go. Willow and I will do all the lifting."

"I think he's bored," I said to Willow, when Uncle Brian had left the boat.

"I'd be bored too if I had to stay with Mum all day," said Willow, with a grin. She pushed through the purple curtain which acted as a door between the shop and the rest of the boat. "Come on, let's get to work. There's a lot to do."

ALMOST TWO HOURS and four aching arms later, Willow and I assessed the situation. The shop space aboard the boat was almost empty of stock, and the shop at the top of the footpath was beginning to look like a real place of business. Uncle Brian certainly knew how to arrange a shop floor, and he'd displayed the stock beautifully, taking great pride in his work as he showed us where everything was.

"Of course, you can always change things around if you like," he said, "but I think it's perfect as it is."

He was right. The shop not only looked magical, but the various herbs and incenses which Uncle Brian had painstakingly separated into scents and uses, gave the shop a magical smell too.

The sales counter was dotted with smaller items and novelty spells which Uncle Brian called impulse purchases, and the crystals and gem stones shone in the sun near the large window.

A shiver of anticipation ran through me as I looked around. It was really happening. I was leaving my shop aboard the boat behind, and starting a new business on land. All that was needed next was a sign to hang above the door outside and furnishings for the interior to make it feel more cozy.

The three of us stood with our backs to the door, taking a silent moment to admire our handiwork, and we all jumped in fright as a loud bang on the window ruined the moment.

"What on earth?" said Uncle Brian, spinning on the spot with his hand on his chest. "I nearly had a heart attack!"

I turned to face the window and immediately recognised the man who was being pressed hard against the glass. His brown overcoat and balding spot on the back of his head gave him away, but if I'd needed anymore proof it was the greengrocer from the shop next door, the cabbage leaves that were being sprinkled liberally over his head would suffice. "It's Mr Jarvis!" I said.

"And it's Felix Round who's attacking him!" noted Willow.

"Oh my!" said Uncle Brian, rushing for the door. "We must help the poor man! Come on, girls, onward into danger!"

The three of us scrambled out of the door in time to see Felix rubbing cabbage leaves in Mr Jarvis's terrified face. "I want celery!" boomed Felix. "I hate cabbage!"

"You've bought it all," stuttered Mr Jarvis, struggling against the hand that gripped him by the throat. "I told you, I'll have more in tomorrow!"

Uncle Brian stepped forward, looking every inch the chivalrous hero. "Unhand that poor man, you oaf!" he ordered. "Immediately. Or I shall not be responsible for my actions!"

"Help me," begged Mr Jarvis. "He's gone mad with the hunger!"

Felix stared at Uncle Brian. He gave a long laugh and stuffed a leaf into Mr Jarvis's mouth, ramming it home with a podgy finger. "What are you three going to do?" said Felix. "You look like you're on your way to a pantomime... and I don't mean as spectators!" He looked Uncle Brian up and down. "What are you wearing, man? You look like a cross between a farmer and a fancy art dealer!"

Uncle Brian pulled his jacket straight and adjusted his hat, the bright red feather that protruded from the rim swaying in the gentle breeze. I glanced down at myself. I didn't think I looked like a character from a pantomime, and anyway, Felix Round was hardly one to speak — he resembled a TV wrestler from the nineteen-seventies — with his belly on show beneath his pie-eating t-shirt, and his angry red face shiny with sweat.

Uncle Brian raised his hand, and lilac sparks danced at the fingertips. "Last chance, you bearded fiend!" he threatened.

"Sod off, you weirdo!" said Felix, his attention back on the important task of stuffing Mr Jarvis's mouth full of cabbage leaves.

Uncle Brain tilted his head and took deep breath. "Oh well, I gave him a chance."

"What are you going to do?" said Willow. "Don't hurt him. Be careful!"

"I won't hurt him," said Uncle Brian, clicking his fingers. "I'm just going to stop him."

The spell crackled in the air and Felix Round let out a long slow gasp as he turned and gazed at Uncle Brian. "What would you have me do, master?" he drawled.

"Unhand that man," said Uncle Brian, winking at me.

Felix released Mr Jarvis who took a few stumbling steps away from Felix and towards the door of his own shop. "What have you done to him?" he said, staring at Uncle Brian. "Why is he doing what you tell him to?"

"I've hypnotised the rogue," said Uncle Brian, showing remarkably quick thinking for a child of Granny's. He pointed at Felix. "Stay right there until I tell you to move," he said.

Felix nodded. "Affirmative, great lord."

"Wow," said Mr Jarvis. "That's amazing!"

"What happened?" I said, as Willow helped Mr Jarvis pick up the produce that had been knocked from his pavement fruit and vegetable display.

"He came in demanding celery," said Mr Jarvis. "He didn't look well. He was sweating and mumbling a lot, and he seemed very angry."

"He's diabetic," I said. "He's probably made himself poorly by not eating enough."

"He grabbed me by the throat when I told him I was all out of celery," continued Mr Jarvis, "and dragged me out of my shop and down the pavement. It was lucky he slammed me into your window, I really think he might have killed me if you three hadn't come out to help."

"The police are already looking for him about one murder," I said, taking my phone from my pocket and dialling nine-nine-nine. "Another one would be a tragedy."

"Him?" said Mr Jarvis. "Did he kill Gerald?"

"Maybe," said Willow. "We don't know yet. The police just want to question him at this stage."

Mr Jarvis put a hand to his throat. "He could have killed me," he murmured.

"This man is wanted for murder?" said Uncle Brian. "Why didn't you tell me? I may not have been so stupidly brave."

"It all happened so quickly," said Willow. "We didn't have time."

I ended the call. "The police will be here in a minute or two," I said. "Erm, Uncle Brian, do you think you'd better… *de-hypnotise* him?"

"In a moment," said Uncle Brian, stepping close to Felix and looking him in the eye. "Answer me truthfully, you violent upstart."

Felix nodded. "I'd do anything for you."

"Have you committed the crime of murder?"

Felix shook his head. "No, oh mightiness."

"He didn't do it," said Uncle Brian. "Nobody can tell a lie when they're controlled by the fingers of Brian Weaver! I declare this man innocent!"

Sirens echoed over the rooftops and the roar of an engine announced the arrival of the police in the street. The car screeched to a halt next to us and two young police women leapt out with their nightsticks drawn.

"Quick," I whispered to Uncle Brian. "The spell."

"Oh yes," said Uncle Brian. "Of course." He muttered something under this breath and Felix gasped as he was released from Uncle Brian's control.

"Is everyone okay?" said one of the police women as her colleague read Felix his rights and cuffed the big mans's hands in front of him.

"I'm not," said Felix. "I feel funny. My head hurts. And I'm so, so hungry."

"That'll teach you," said Mr Jarvis, picking up ruined peaches from the gutter. "Attacking a man in his own shop like that!" He pointed at Uncle Brian. "That man deserves a medal, officer," he said to the policewoman. "Or a TV show at least. I've never seen anything like it. He hypnotised him and made him do what he told him to. It was extraordinary."

Uncle Brain beamed. "It was my pleasure," he

said with a low bow. "A medal is unwarranted, but a TV show would be splendid. Imagine it — a Weaver on the television!"

"Hypnotised him, you say?" said the shortest of the two policewomen. "Do you think you could help me stop smoking?"

Uncle Brain adjusted his silk cravat. "My dear," he said. "I could definitely stop you from smoking."

"What about eating?" said the other policewoman, guiding Felix into the backseat of the car. "Can you help me get beach body ready for my holiday?"

"Of course," said Uncle Brian. "I am after all, a hypnotist." He took a moleskin notepad and fountain pen from his pocket and scribbled his phone number on a sheet of paper. He ripped it from the book and handed it to the woman who was keen to stop smoking. "Telephone me for an appointment," he said.

The policewomen thanked him and sped off with their prisoner.

"What are you doing?" I said under my breath, as Willow helped Mr Jarvis back inside his shop. "You can't pretend to hypnotise people and use magic on them! It's immoral and probably dangerous!"

"Of course I can" said Uncle Brian. "It's a genius idea, I'm not sure why I've never thought of it before."

I didn't bother arguing. It was never worth arguing with a Weaver. When a Weaver had made a decision, it was practically set in stone. "What spell was that, anyway?" I said instead. "It was quite impressive, although it was strange how he called you his mightiness."

"A spell of subservient adoration," said Uncle Brian. "It's very useful. You should learn it. It can open all sorts of doors for you. I eat for free in a lot of London's swankiest restaurants, thanks to that little spell."

A squeal of tyres and the roar of a powerful engine broke the silence in the street, and I watched in disbelief as a black Range Rover careered around the corner on the wrong side of the road.

"Who's that?" said Uncle Brian. "That's a really nice motor, and a very proficient driver!"

"That's your mother," I said, taking two steps backwards as the large four-by-four came to a screeching halt next to us.

Willow rushed out of the greengrocer's shop as Granny revved the engine and rolled down the tinted window. She waved a hand at us, her face ashen. "Quick. Jump in, I need help. Boris has been kidnapped!" she said.

CHAPTER TWELVE

"*W*hat do you mean kidnapped?" I asked, as Granny took a sharp left turn, sending me and Willow sprawling in the back seat. Uncle Brian sat in the front with Granny, and he put his hand over his eyes as Granny barely avoided slamming the Range Rover into the postbox outside the coffee pot café.

"Slow down," said Willow. "Someone will get hurt!"

Granny swung the Range Rover into Church Street. "My Boris is probably undergoing all sorts of hideous experiments and tests as we speak. I can't afford to slow down. I need to get to my goat. He needs me!"

"The famous talking goat?" said Uncle Brian, holding on tight as the car rolled to the right. "I'm yet to meet him, but I'm more than ready to help him in his hour of need! Who's kidnapped him, Mother? And for what manner of nefarious reason?"

"You're such a good boy, Brian," said Granny, slamming the brakes on as a lollipop woman stepped into the highway to allow a gaggle of chocolate and candy eating children to cross the road. "Nobody would guess you were so terribly oppressed. You have such a kind heart! Boris will be thrilled to meet you if we can ever rescue him."

Willow rolled her eyes as Granny gave the engine a burst of revs and pulled away with a squeal of rubber on tarmac. "Who's taken Boris, Granny?" she said.

"Those bastards from the animal welfare department," said Granny. "I got home with the new wheels and found a note on my door. They say they have reason to believe he was the goat present at the quarry fire, and they say he's been mistreated. They've taken him to Applehill veterinary centre for tests! I pray to all that is holy and sacred that they don't still take an animal's temperature by sticking a thermometer up the jacksy! Can you imagine Boris allowing anybody to do that? He's such a proud fellow — he wouldn't let *anybody* near that private spot, let alone a total stranger who kidnapped him!"

Granny made a right turn onto Applehill and gunned the engine with a heavy foot. The Range

Rover lurched forward and accelerated quickly up the steep hill towards the red brick building which sat at the peak.

The car park was nearly empty, and Granny brought the car to a halt outside the veterinary centre doors. "Quickly," she said, opening her door and sliding out. "We've no time to waste, and as matriarch of the Weaver family, I grant each of you permission to use magic during operation *free Boris*. He must be rescued no matter what! I'm willing to rack up fatalities if need be — we'll call it collateral damage."

"No one's getting hurt," I said, as Brian rolled up his sleeves and flexed his fingers. "Calm down. We'll just go inside and find out what's happening. I'm sure Boris is fine, and we'll have him home in no time. Everything will be okay. It always is."

Granny led the way along the short path and pushed through the doors into the building. The reception desk was devoid of staff, and three upturned chairs in the waiting room were the first clue that maybe everything wasn't fine after all.

A raised voice came from the corridor to our left, and Granny followed it with the eagerness of a dog on the scent of a fox. Uncle Brian followed her as far as the large animal weighing scales, and took a moment out of his busy schedule to stand on them. "Good gracious me!" he said. "No wonder my boxers are pinching my man eggs! I've put on six pounds since I last weighed!"

"Well, I think you look truly wonderful, my darling," said Granny. "I always said you carried your weight better than that sister of yours. A few extra pounds make you look mayoral and healthy. Maggie just balloons into a big wrinkly mess when she goes over two-hundred-and-fifty."

Another raised voice came from behind a door further along the corridor. "This way!" said Granny.

A woman's scream increased the urgency of the situation, and I quickened my pace as Granny reached the door and swung it open with a push. "What the devil?" she shouted. "What's happening in here? Boris, my gentle goat, are you okay?"

Willow rushed into the room behind Granny, and Uncle Brian and I entered together, jut as a woman screamed again. "Please make it stop!" she begged. "I don't know what's happening. I'm scared!"

The scene in the room was one of complete madness. Pain blossomed in my bottom lip as I bit into it, and even Uncle Brian seemed shocked. He took a step backwards and lowered himself into a plastic chair, loosening his cravat and taking deep breaths as he fanned himself with his hat.

A group of people stood huddled together in the furthest corner from the door. Some held animal crates, and others held onto leashes with terrified dogs at the ends of them. Two of the people wore white coats, and one of them, a woman with a stethoscope around her neck, was crying uncontrollably.

Boris stood in front of the captive people, baring his teeth and snapping at the air whenever somebody moved. A golden labrador took a tentative step towards Boris, but cowered against its owner's legs when Boris let out a blood curling scream. "Get back in line you filthy animal!"

"Help us," said a man holding a tiny lap dog close to his chest. "He rounded us all up like a dog rounds up sheep, and trapped us in this room. He bit me on the buttock, I'll need a tetanus jab!"

The trembling woman next to him pointed a finger at Boris. "It speaks too," she murmured. "The goat speaks! I only came here to get worming tablets for my cat, and now I'm trapped in a horrific nightmare." She looked at the floor. "I took acid in the seventies, maybe it's come back to haunt me."

Granny dropped to her knees next to Boris. "My poor, poor Boris," she said, wrapping an arm around his neck. "What have they done to you?"

"Gladys," said Boris, quite calmly considering the circumstances. "I have a thermometer inserted where the sun doesn't shine. Be so good as to remove it for me, would you? Ive tried, but I can't quite get my mouth around that far, and I've been hesitant to take my eye off these people. One of them has already tried to inject me with what I can only imagine is a sedative of some description. Who knows what they'll do to me if they get the chance."

"I only wanted some eyedrops for my gerbil," said a tall wiry man with thick black rimmed glasses. "I just want to go home. I won't hurt you, Boris."

"I'm sorry you've been dragged into this, Nigel," said Boris. "But I had to take you all hostage until help arrived. I knew Gladys would come for me eventually, it was only a matter of waiting long enough."

"How do you know his name is Nigel, Boris?" said Willow.

"He did a meet and greet," said a young girl dressed in the green uniform of an animal nurse. "He made us tell him our full names, starsigns, and our ambitions."

Boris snapped at the leg of a man as he attempted to move towards a table with a telephone on it. "Get back, Larry," he growled. "Or you'll never see the Niagara Falls."

Granny pointed at a table. "Penelope," she said, "pass me something I can use to pull this thermometer from out of Boris. There's barely any of it visible. It's really gone deep, Boris. It can't be comfortable for you."

I rifled through a tray of medical implements and settled on a pair of forceps. Granny took them from me and held Boris still as she carefully slid the glass tube from his rear end.

Boris let out a contented moan of pleasure as the thermometer left his body, and snarled at one of the vets. "I will *never* forgive you," he said. "You took my dignity from me."

Granny stood up and stared at Boris's prisoners. "You should be ashamed," she said. "Stealing a goat from his own home and forcing him to endure horrific medical experiments."

"We were worried about him," said a woman. "We followed the footsteps of a goat that was involved in an incident in a quarry, and they led to your home. We needed to make sure he wasn't being mistreated. The last time he was seen he was wearing a balaclava, and that's animal cruelty."

"As you can see, he's perfectly fine," said Granny. "I do not mistreat him."

"He talks," said a female vet. "That's not fine. There's something very wrong about this whole situation, and we need to get to the bottom of it, so if you'd just allow us to do our jobs, we can find out what's wrong with the poor animal."

Uncle Brian had recovered, and carefully placed his hat on his head as he stood up. "Mother, would you like me to work a little magic?" he said, wriggling the fingers on both hands. "I think these people need to forget what they saw here today."

Granny clapped. "Go on, son," she said. "Give them what for! Show them who's boss!"

Sparks crackled at Brian's fingertips, and a woman made a break for the door, clutching a basket which contained an injured crow.

"Stop right there, Mrs Oliver!" said Boris. "It will be easier if you don't resist."

"Mrs Oliver?" I said. "The birdwatcher? The woman who kept complaining about Gerald Timkins?"

The woman's face froze in an expression midway between a smile and a scowl. "Yes that's me, and I'm still clearing up his barbaric mess. I found this young crow today with a broken wing and pellets embedded in its abdomen. I'm sorry about what happened to him, but I'm not sorry he can't shoot at defenceless birds anymore. Who knows? Maybe he had it coming. Anyway, the police have already spoken to me about it. They had the audacity to ask if I knew anything. I told them the truth. I didn't see anything or hear anything, and that's the end of the matter."

Uncle Brian waved his hand in the air, trailing bright sparks behind it which mesmerised the crowd of people huddled in the corner. "What are you?" said one of them. "Who are you people, and why can that goat talk?"

Mrs Oliver made another panicked attempt at reaching the door, and Brian cast his spell. The air in the room seemed to heat up, and my eardrums popped as the people huddled in the corner sighed in unison and froze in position.

"Very good, Brian," said Granny, getting to her knees in front of the male vet.

"What are you doing?" gasped Willow. "Pull his trousers back up and put that thermometer down!"

"I'm just repaying him," said Granny, grasping a buttock and pulling it aside. "Let's see how he likes a glass tube in *his* bottom."

"Boris," I whispered. "Please stop her. Nothing good can come from this!"

Boris snorted his contempt. "He deserves it."

"I'll buy you a bottle of brandy every week for a month," I negotiated.

"And a packet of cigars?"

I nodded. "Deal. Just make her stop, she hasn't even put any lube on it!"

"Gladys," said Boris. "Stop that. He was only doing his job. Two wrongs don't make a right."

"But, Boris," said Granny, taking aim. "I need my revenge. You know it's my weakness."

Boris stepped slowly towards Granny and placed a hoof on her shoulder. "Your revenge will be knowing you're a better person than he is, Gladys."

Granny hesitated, but released the buttock and withdrew the tip of the thermometer from near catastrophe. "Can I leave his trousers and underwear around his feet? That will steady my lust for revenge."

I shrugged and Willow nodded. "Yes," said Boris. "Leave him as he is."

"Okay, Brian," said Granny. "Make them all forget what happened."

"Wait," said Willow as Uncle Brian lifted his hand. "Can you ask Mrs Oliver if she killed Gerald Timkins? You know, the same way you asked Felix Round if he was a murderer? Let's be sure she's innocent while we've got her trapped here."

Brain smiled. "Of course I can," he said. He waved his right hand in front of Mrs Oliver's face as his left hand kept the other people under control. "Did you murder a man?" he said. "Speak the truth and speak it freely!"

"No," mumbled Mrs Oliver. "I've not killed a man."

"Does she know anything about it at all?" I said.

"Tell me what you know about Gerald's death," said Uncle Brian.

"Nothing," said Mrs Oliver. "But you should ask the scarecrow making man."

"Who?" said Uncle Brian.

"The scarecrow man," said Mrs Oliver. "He told me he was angry with Gerald."

"Did you tell the police?" said Uncle Brian.

"No," said Mrs Oliver. "I won't help the police.

Gerald Timkins had it coming. He shot innocent animals, and someone shot him. It's poetic justice."

"Who's the scarecrow making man?" said Uncle Brian.

Mrs Oliver furrowed her brow and groaned.

"Hurry," said Granny. "You can't keep two spells going at the same time like this Brian, they're beginning to weaken."

Granny was right. The other people in the room were starting to regain some control over themselves. One woman moved her nose and another blinked. The vet with his dignity around his ankles began bending at the waist to reach for his trousers.

Uncle Brian nodded. "Sorry, girls," he said, speaking to me and Willow. "I can't ask her anymore questions." He clicked his fingers and everybody fell still again, including Mrs Oliver. "You'll all wake up in three minutes," said Uncle Brian. "And have no memory of what's happened here today. You'll forget about goats and mistreatment, and everyone will think it's perfectly normal to all be in this room together. They'll be suspicions as to why the strange male vet has his tackle on display, but you'll carry on with your day as if nothing's happened." IIe clicked his fingers again. "We've got three minutes," he said.

Granny rubbed her hands together in glee. "Everybody into the car," she said. "I've always wanted to be a getaway driver!"

CHAPTER THIRTEEN

"*I* look ridiculous," I said. "Surely I can wear shoes without heels. Barney won't care."

Willow seemed more excited than I was about the fact that I was going out for a meal with Barney. She'd almost forced me to borrow one of her dresses and a pair of matching shoes.

"Penny," said Willow. "You're below average height for a woman, and Barney is ridiculously tall — for a man *or* a woman. There's nothing wrong with adding a couple of inches to your height. You don't want to strain your back when it's time to snog him, do you?"

Willow expertly avoided the make-up brush I threw at her. "There'll be no kissing, thank you very much! We're just friends. Anyway. Barney is a gentlemen. He wouldn't expect me to kiss him on a first date."

Susie looked up from her laptop. "So it *is* a date!"

"Who rattled your cage?" I laughed, sitting down to take the strain off my calves. Heels may have added a little height, but they certainly couldn't be described as comfort wear. "I thought you were supposed to be doing some investigative journalism, not helping my sister tease me."

Susie tapped at her keyboard. "There's nothing about scarecrow making men," she said. "According to google, farmers make their own scarecrows. There used to be people who made them for a living, but the art died out years ago. Maybe Mrs Oliver got muddled up."

"Maybe," I said. "I'll tell Barney though. It might mean something to him."

I tugged the hem of the black dress a little further down my thigh. I was sure it was too short, but both Susie and Willow assured me it was fine. Yes, they enjoyed teasing me, but neither of them would see me going out in a dress which looked terrible on me. I trusted them.

My hair was gathered high on my head and held in position by numerous hairpins which Willow had studiously applied, and the matching earring and necklace set which Mum had given me on my eighteenth birthday twinkled in the light as I checked my makeup in my compact mirror. Mum had insisted the diamonds had been bought from a shop in our world, but I was convinced they'd come from the haven. It seemed impossible that earthly diamonds could shine with so many colours. They even looked magical.

Wherever they were from, they only came out on very special occasions, and I classed the meal with Barney as being a very special occasion. Not only was it a chance for the two of us to share some time alone — it was also the first time I'd be seeing Barney since he'd found out I was a witch. It was a new situation for us both and things could get awkward, and I at least wanted to look nice in case Barney said something which made me angry enough to storm out of the restaurant.

Willow accompanied me along the path into town to wait for the taxi. We stood outside our shop and made plans for the sign which would hang outside and make the shop official.

"Don't be late home and don't do anything I wouldn't do," joked Willow as the taxi appeared at the end of Bridge Street.

Barney climbed from the car and opened the door for me, much to Willow's delight. "Aww, that's nice of you. Barney," she said. "And I must say — you do scrub up well. Look at you, Wickford's very own James Bond! I don't think I've ever seen you in a suit."

Barney blushed, ignoring the compliment. We weren't so different, me and him — neither of us dealt very well with compliments or praise. A compliment may have made Barney blush, but they made my skin crawl and my jaw tighten. Especially if I didn't feel good about myself.

"You look really nice, Penny," Barney said, helping me balance on my heels as I climbed into the back of the car. "Really pretty."

Instead of the familiar awkwardness, Barney's genuine compliment made me smile. "Thank you," I said, as Barney climbed in beside me. "You don't look too bad yourself."

He didn't look in the least bit bad. In fact, he looked amazing. The suit he wore fitted him better than any other clothes I'd ever seen him wear, and he'd obviously taken time to make his hair look stylishly messy. I'd be proud to walk into a restaurant with him.

Willow stood on the pavement waving as the taxi pulled away, and Barney reached between his feet and handed me a bouquet of flowers which he'd been hiding. "I wasn't sure when to give them to you," he said. "Before or after the meal. I've never really given a woman flowers before, apart from my Mum and Nan obviously. But I think that's different. I mean —"

Barney's face tightened with anxiety, and I

quietened him with a kiss on his cheek. "They're really lovely, Barney," I said. "Thank you."

"I wanted to add a flower that would suit you, some sort of witchcraft flower, like hemlock or something, but the woman in the shop looked at me like I was mad. She put a sprig of elderflower in though. I think that's supposed to be magical, isn't it?"

I put a finger to my lips and nodded at the back of the driver's head. "Don't talk about that here," I said. "Wait until the restaurant. It'll be more private."

BARNEY HAD BOOKED the table in advance, and he'd chosen the perfect table for a couple who required privacy. As the name suggested, The *Cosy Cucina* was not a large restaurant, and most of the dozen or so tables had couples or small families already seated at them.

The waiter led us to a secluded cubical table in a corner near the large window. The view across the countryside was breathtaking even in the dying light, and the canal was still visible in the distance as the sun gave way to the moon.

Barney ordered us some wine, and I licked my lips as the aroma of garlic and mussels flooding from the kitchen made my mouth water. We ordered our meals, and with a full wine glass each, Barney's bottom lip already staining red from just a few small sips, I looked him in the eye. "You're taking the whole thing very well, Barney," I said, "I'd have thought you'd have had a lot of questions for me. I know I probably would if *I'd* just found out that witches existed."

"Of course I have questions," said Barney, breaking a small piece of bread from one of the rolls in the wicker basket in the centre of the round table. "But I understand how it is for you, Penny. And Susie, Willow, and erm.. Boris were very patient with me. When I had to rush off to work and leave you in that *trance* in your bed, I was scared and I wanted to know everything. It took all my self control to stay away from you until now, but I thought you'd need to think about things just as much as I needed to. It's not everyday your secret is laid bare like it was that night at the meal. It must have been very difficult for you too."

It had been difficult, but I'd have thought what Barney had gone through would have been worse. "It was," I said. "But I'm happy that you know the truth. I just need to know that you can handle the truth, Barney. Finding out that witches exist must have turned your world upside down. I know some people wouldn't be able to handle it."

"Can I handle knowing that witches exist and that the woman who's sitting opposite me sharing a bottle of wine can do magic? Hell, yeah, I can handle that! It's awesome, Penny, and Susie told me how your magic helped with the Sam Hedgewick case. Imagine it — I've got a witch as a... friend, who can solve crimes! It's amazing."

I took a long gulp of wine. "I can't really solve crimes, Barney. I can help you, but the leg work still needs to be done by the police."

We stopped speaking as the waiter slid our starters in front of us. Seared scallops for Barney, and mussels with white wine sauce for me. I knew that drinking red wine with fish went against every piece of food advice I'd ever read or been given, but it seemed that Barney's and my relationship was breaking a lot of normal conventions. Drinking the wrong wine with a meal was the least of them.

"How do you do it, Penny?" said Barney. "I mean how do you actually do it... like how do you cast a spell or whatever it is you do?"

"Wiggle your fingers on your left hand," I said.

Barney gave me an enquiring look, but laid his fork down and did as I'd asked.

"How did you do that, Barney?" I said. "How did you wiggle your fingers?"

"I don't know. I thought about doing it and it just happened."

"That's how magic works" I said. "When you first learn a new spell it takes a little more effort, but after that, it's just a case of thinking about what you want to do. Just like wiggling your fingers."

Barney asked me more questions, and I answered each one as honestly as I could. We were onto the subject of the haven by the time Barney's lamb shank with rosemary gravy and my paella had arrived at the table.

"You can go to the haven, but you haven't gone yet?" said Barney. "Why?"

"I've waited so long," I said. "I can wait a day or two longer while Mum arranges a simple ceremony for me. It would be unfair of me to enter without Mum. She'd take it very badly, and to be honest, I'm a little nervous about going alone."

Barney nodded and put a hand to his head. He rubbed his temple with two fingers and winced. "Ouch," he said. "I've had a terrible headache all day. It's wearing off though. Thanks to the wine, I think."

"It's because of the spell you had cast on you," I said. "It will go away soon enough."

"What spell," said Barney. "You stopped them casting one, remember?"

I sipped my wine. "The spell that Willow cast on you to make you forget. At Granny's cottage. That was powerful magic, it was bound to give you a headache."

"What are you talking about?" said Barney,

placing his glass on the table and staring at me. "What spell at Granny's? Making me forget what?"

I swallowed hard. I'd assumed that Willow, Boris, and Susie had told him everything... including the fact that we'd wiped his memory clean. "Nothing," I said, my cheeks warming from the lie. "I've had too much wine."

"Penny," said Barney. "I'll ask you once more, and I'd like to think you trust me enough to give me an honest answer. What spell at Granny's?"

I dabbed my mouth with a napkin. "You came to Granny's house to investigate an arson, Barney, remember?"

He nodded. "Of course I do, everything was okay. I crossed your grandmother out of my book and told Sergeant Cooper she had nothing to do with it. Or that goat of hers. It seems quite weird now I know the goat can speak though, but I definitely found nothing amiss at Ashwood cottage."

"It didn't quite go down like that," I said.

"How did it go down then, Penny? What happened to me."

"You'll be angry," I said, "and we probably broke the law too. How will you deal with that?"

"Just tell me," said Barney. "I'll deal with it the same way I deal with everything... calmly and rationally."

"I can do better than tell you," I said. "I can show you. If you trust me to cast a spell on you, that is."

After watching Willow cast the spell, I'd taken the time to learn it myself. It was simple to learn a spell from Granny's spell book. A spell was s series of numbers, letters, and symbols, which imprinted themselves onto a witches mind when she read them. It had taken me less than a minute to learn the spell Willow had cast, and I'd spent a further half an hour learning more spells, including one which could bring back memories.

"Do it," said Barney. "Make me remember."

"Here?" I said. "It might be too public here, Barney. You might have a shock when you remember what happened."

Barney narrowed his eyes. "Just do it," he said.

I glanced around the room. The other customers were either preoccupied with eating, or deep in conversation with their dining companions.

"Okay," I said. "Prepare yourself. I'm not sure how it will work."

Barney gripped the edge of the table with both hands. "Go for it. I'm ready. I want to know what you did to me, and why you did it to me."

The spell came easily. I sucked a little air between my lips and tasted copper in my mouth. The spell tingled in my fingertips, and I hid my hands beneath the table as I clicked my fingers.

Barney closed his eyes and gasped, the table rocked a little as he tightened his grip on it, and I put my hand on one of his. "It's okay," I said. "You're safe."

"Goat in garden," he mumbled. "Cigar smoke in strange backroom. No one in cottage smokes though."

"That's it," I said, unsure if he could hear me. "Let the memories come back slowly."

Barney smiled, his eyes still closed. "Penny's bottom on the stairs in front of me. Nice. Mustn't touch though, however tempting."

I wondered why I was blushing — Barney had his eyes closed and I doubted he had any idea about what he was saying. There was no reason to be embarrassed, but my cheeks burned hot nonetheless.

"Mad Gladys Weaver," murmured Barney. "Look in her bedroom. Why does she keep a baseball bat under her bed? None of my business. It's not illegal. Forget what you saw in her top drawer — never think of it again — it might mentally scar you. Leave Barney... go and look in next bedroom."

I promised myself I'd never look in Granny's top drawer, however tempted I was, and watched Barney's face closely. The important part was coming up. He was about to remember discovering Charleston Huang's hiding place.

"What's in the corner?" said Barney, his voice becoming louder. "A man! In the corner! Get out!"

Barney's eyes snapped open and he stared through me. "Come out with your hands up!" he shouted, standing up and knocking the bread basket off the table. "Light-shade on his head! Chinese fellow in the corner! Is he dead?"

People stopped eating and lowered their cutlery as a waiter scampered towards us, placing the tray he was carrying on the nearest table and putting his hand on Barney's back. "No dead Chinese man in here," he said in broken English. "This Italian restaurant! No dead men at all in corner!"

Barney ignored him. "Am I in heaven?"

"No, sir," said the waiter. "Food good here, but this not heaven!"

I attempted to stop the spell, but it seemed that when the memories which Willow had purged from Barney's mind had been replaced by my spell, there was nothing to do but let it run its course and wait for Barney to recover.

"He's okay," I said, as the waiter looked in Barney's wine glass, possibly for drugs. "He's just very tired."

"Too much wine?" said the waiter. He looked Barney up and down. "He very tall man. Should be able to drink lots."

"Yes, he is tall," I said. "But he doesn't drink very often."

Barney laughed, his eyes closed again. "I'll only pay for half of the meal! Perfect!"

"No, sir," said the waiter. "Not perfect. You pay full price."

Barney gasped, and the waiter took a hurried step away from him.

"Are you alright?" I said, as colour flooded Barney's cheeks.

Barney sat down and waved at the spectators he'd acquired. "Show's over," he laughed.

The waiter smiled at Barney. "You fine now, sir?" he said.

"Everything's fine," said Barney. "Thank you."

When the other diners had started eating again, and the bread and basket had been picked up from the floor, the waiter retrieved his tray and continued with his business.

I leaned across the table. "I'm so sorry, Barney," I said. "I feel awful about everything that happened at Granny's, and now I've put you in terrible position — you have to decide whether you're going to charge Granny with arson or not, now you know the truth."

"Charge Gladys?" said Barney, his eyes sparkling. "Of course not. How can I possibly apply laws which are meant for humans, to witches? I understand everything now... that spell did more than give me my memories back... it filled in the blanks too. I know who Charleston Huang is and I know why Gladys and Boris burnt that car. They had to protect themselves. The secret is safe with me, Penny. You have my word."

"I'd have thought you'd have been angrier," I said. "We stole your memories."

"For a valid reason," said Barney. "And anyway, how could I be angry? I was just given a beautiful memory."

"What on earth was beautiful about what happened to you in that cottage?" I said. "Scary, yes. Hideous, maybe. Beautiful — I'm just not seeing it."

Barney took my hand in his. "When Willow asked you if you wanted me to forget about the meal, you said no. You said you wanted to come with me, and you even offered to pay half which was a lovely gesture! I've never been happier, Penny. I wondered if you were just coming for a meal with me out of pity, but now I know the truth, and it's the best feeling I've ever had. It certainly takes the sting out of the shame I feel for the comment I made about your bottom."

I laughed. "You remember saying that?"

Barney nodded. "I remember everything that happened in your grandmother's cottage, and to my shame…everything that just happened here — it will be a long time before I eat in this restaurant again." He paused momentarily, and squeezed my hand. "There's no secrets between us anymore, is there, Penny?"

"I wish the comment about my bottom was still a secret, Barney," I giggled. "But no, as far as I'm concerned there are no more secrets between us."

Barney leaned across the table, and despite a few of the other customers and the waiter still watching us, I sat forward in my seat, smiled at him, and allowed him to kiss me.

It was how I'd imagined it would be, and the fluttering in my belly stayed with me long after Barney had pulled his lips from mine and ordered dessert.

CHAPTER FOURTEEN

"The scarecrow man," said Willow, seemingly out of nowhere.

I looked up from the box of novelty spells I was sorting through. "What about him? I told Barney last night and he said he wasn't aware of anyone who makes scarecrows. He's asking around though, but because we got the information from Mrs Oliver by using magic, he has to be careful what he says."

Willow placed a cast iron cauldron on a low display shelf near the door. "You told Barney about what happened in the vets?"

"Yes," I said. "There are no secrets between us anymore."

"What did he say?"

"He didn't really want to talk about the Gerald Timkins case. He was more interested in the fact that

I'm a witch, Willow, but he laughed and asked how Boris was after his ordeal... he's very taken with him. He wants a boys night in... just him, Boris, and a bottle of brandy."

Willow smiled. "I can't think of anything that could go wrong with that," she said. "Not a thing at all."

"My thoughts precisely," I said, allowing myself a giggle as I pictured Boris and Barney drinking into the small hours of the morning. "But Barney's a little like me. He doesn't have many friends. It will be nice for him to be able to relax and have some fun with Boris."

Willow stood up and joined me at the sales counter, flipping through a brochure from the sign writing company we'd chosen to make the sign for the shop. "As I was saying," she said. "The scarecrow man."

"And as I said — what about him?"

"Remember that pick-up truck? The one that nearly knocked us down in the lane on the way to Granny's?"

I nodded, realisation dawning. "Yes, I do. The one that seemed to be in a real hurry, probably around the time Gerald was killed!"

"The one that dropped old clothes and straw from the back," added Willow. "It doesn't take a huge leap of faith to suggest that he might be the scarecrow man, does it?"

I already had my phone to my ear. "I'll tell Barney," I said. "The police are still questioning Felix Round, but Barney doesn't think he did it. He has a strong alibi — he said he was at a yoga class to help stretch his stomach for the pie eating competition. Barney's checking it out."

"Tell him I remembered it," said Willow. "I could do with a little praise."

Barney answered the phone. "Hi," I said, blushing as Willow doodled a heart on the notepad next to her, writing *Penny luvs Barney*, inside it.

I told Barney what had happened in the lane and explained our suspicions, adding that it had been Willow's suggestion, much to her delight. "I don't," I said, when Barney asked if I remembered a registration plate number. "Maybe willow does."

Willow was no help either, and Barney ended the call with only a vague description of the pick-up truck and driver to help with his investigation.

"He's checking out CCTV footage in town," I said, "looking for the pick-up, but there's not many cameras. He says the police are releasing Felix this morning, too. His alibi checks out, and Mr Jarvis doesn't want to press charges either."

"I was sure he'd done it," said Willow. "He seemed so angry."

"It's the quiet ones you have to watch out for," I

said. "According to Granny, but she's not quiet and you have to look out for her."

Willow laughed, and glanced at her watch. "Speaking of Granny, we'd better lock up the shop and get going. She wants us there by ten o'clock."

Willow switched off the lights and I closed the door behind us. The shop was going to be opened officially when our new sign had been delivered and fitted, and Willow and I were both excited about running a business together. "Granny can't demand our presence when the shop is officially open," I said, locking the door. "We can't just open and close when we feel like it. We'll get a terrible reputation."

Willow nodded. "Of course, but you must admit you want to go to Granny's this morning, though? I know I do."

I slipped the keys into my short's pocket. "I do too," I admitted. "I'm intrigued about —"

"Girls! Could I have a moment of your time please?"

The woman's voice cut me off mid sentence, and Willow and I turned to see a short woman running across the road towards us.

"Mrs Round," said Willow.

"Im sorry to bother you both," said the tiny woman with the big hair. "But I wanted to apologise for my husband's behaviour outside your shop. I've already apologised to Mr Jarvis, and he kindly agreed to drop the charges of assault against Felix. I've been told that you two and a man had to come outside and stop Felix from hurting poor Mr Jarvis. A hypnotist, a policewoman told me?"

"Yes, that was our uncle," I said. "But there's no need to apologise. We're just happy that Felix is okay, and that the police have cleared him of murder. It can't be easy to have that sort of accusation hanging around your neck."

Mrs Round shook her head and offered us a narrow smile. "Murder and Felix don't even belong in the same sentence," she said. "He's normally as mild mannered as a stoned vicar, but when it's pie eating competition time, he turns into another man completely — not violent though, you understand? Just hungry and grumpy. What he did to Mr Jarvis was completely out of character for him. It's his health, he really needs to stop with these stupid food eating competitions before they kill him."

"Is he still taking part in the pie eating competition?" said Willow. "After what's happened?"

"Yes," said Mrs Round, wiping a tear from the corner of her eye, her green nail polish matching her eye shadow perfectly. "He says if he wins it will be his last one. He'll have set a new record, and he'll be happy. I've got my fingers crossed for him, I don't think he'll be alive in two years time if he carries on eating the way he does. The doctor says he needs to make changes now."

"We'll cross our fingers for him too," I offered.

Mrs Round smiled. "Thank you," she said. "It's such a shame that the competition has been overshadowed by the death of The Tank, though. Felix had a lot of respect for Gerald, even though it may not have seemed like it sometimes. It really is awful. All the money that's raised this year is going to his wife."

"I'm sure Sandra will be grateful," I said.

"Poor lady," said Mrs Round. "I can't imagine what it must be like for a woman to lose her husband. I don't know what I'd do without Felix. That's what makes me so angry about this whole eating for competitions nonsense. He doesn't seem to care that if he drops dead from a heart attack he'll be leaving me on my own."

I glanced at my phone, trying not to seem rude, but aware that Granny would be waiting for me and Willow to arrive. "I'm really sorry," I said. "We have to be somewhere. We'll see you at the pie eating competition, though. We'll be there to support Felix."

GRANNY TAPPED her watch as Willow and I strolled into the kitchen. "What time do you call this? I said ten o'clock sharp, not seven minutes past ten."

"Sorry, Granny," said Willow. "We got held up, but we're here now. That's all that matters isn't it?"

Granny stood up. "I suppose so. Come on then girls, Boris is in his study writing his blog. Let's go and ask him about this photograph."

Granny retrieved the black and white photograph of the ballet dancer from her apron pocket, and Willow's eyes lit up. "I thought you weren't going to wear the apron when you got the Range Rover," she said with a grin, pointing through the window at the large black car. "You're lower middle class now, aren't you?"

"I said I wouldn't wear it when I go somewhere," said Granny. "Of course I'm going to wear it at home — it's very handy. You girls should try one. I got my first apron at eighteen, and I've never looked back."

Granny took two steps towards the door, her foot-steps like somebody hammering a nail.

"Heavens, Granny!" said Willow. "You're wearing your clogs, I see. They're very loud."

"Aren't they lovely, though?" said Granny, lifting one foot for us to inspect. "They fit perfectly, and Boris says they make me look very continental. My back feels better too... I walk with a far straighter gait, don't you think?"

"Maybe, but you sound like a horse on this slate floor, Granny," I said.

"They're better on carpet, I'll be the first to

admit," said Granny, clip clopping through the kitchen.

Granny led us to Boris's closed study door and knocked on it gently "Let me do the talking," she said, as Boris called us in. "I'm a little more sensitive than you pair. You two would go at it like a bull in a china shop, and personal family matters like this require a little more finesse and understanding — such as I can offer."

Willow tittered, and I rolled my eyes. "Why did you want us here then, Granny?" I said. "You could have asked him on your own."

"Moral support," said Granny, "and I know you two are just as nosy as me."

Boris nodded a greeting as we entered, and spoke into the microphone next to his laptop. "Go to sleep," he said. The voice activation software did as it was told, and Boris's laptop screen flickered and turned black. "My three favourite ladies," he said, turning around on his cushion until he faced us. "Something tells me you haven't interrupted me to ask how my blog is going…. although it's going very well, thank you. I've got quite a fanbase building, and the Golden Wok delivers free food for me and Gladys once a week in return for me advertising them."

"Very nice it is too," said Granny. "I ate some squid last time didn't I, Boris? Even though I didn't want to!"

"You did, Gladys," verified Boris.

Granny puffed out her chest. "Boris said it's good to try new foods, and that he was very proud of me, didn't you, Boris?"

Boris chuckled. "I did indeed, Gladys. I did indeed. You're a brave woman. Not everybody would try squid."

"Erm… well done, Granny," I said. "I suppose." I pointed at the photograph in her hand. "Go on then, show him."

"Show me what?" said Boris. "What's that you have there, Gladys? A photograph? That frame looks familiar. Let me see it."

Granny turned the picture around, and Boris gave a gentle sigh. "It's Nanna Chang-Chang when she was young. She was a beautiful woman and an expert ballet dancer. Those clogs you're wearing were hers, Gladys. She used them to improve her posture and strengthen her feet." Boris tilted his head and twitched an ear. "Why do you have that picture? I only asked you too bring me the photograph of my parents, which I'm very grateful for incidentally."

The other photograph we'd brought back from Charleston's home was on the mantelpiece over-looking Boris's coffee table desk. His mother and father were pictured outside, beneath a large tree, and both of them looked happy.

Boris gazed up at the picture of his parents.

"Nanna Chang-Chang didn't pass her dancing skills down to her daughter though — my mother had two left feet and no rhythm whatsoever."

"Boris," said Granny, sitting on the sofa and laying the picture on her lap. "I have this picture because I recognise the woman in it. In fact, I knew Chang-Chang personally... not very well, but I did know her."

"How did you know her, Gladys?" said Boris. "She died when I was ten, she got ill."

A tear ran the length of a thick hair near Boris's eye, and Granny wiped it away with a thumb. "Did you ever think she was special, Boris?" she said. "I mean differently special."

"Of course she was special," said Boris. "She was Nanna. She was a wonderful woman. Kind and considerate, but you didn't want to cross her, oh no! She had a vicious tongue in her mouth and she knew how to use it. She didn't speak English very well, but you got the meaning from her facial expressions — she was very elastic in the face department, and very gifted at impressions too. My mother told me she could do a perfect Chairman Mao, although she did get in trouble for it once or twice."

Granny sighed. She was thinking... looking for the right words to tell Boris he came from magical ancestors. I sat next to her and put my hand on her forearm. "Tell him, Granny," I said. "Just be honest."

Boris sat higher on his cushion. "Tell me what, Gladys?"

"Boris, I don't know how to tell you, or how it say it." Granny put her hand on Boris's shoulder and looked him in the eyes. "Oh sod it!" she said. "Boris, your grandmother was a witch."

The tip of Boris's tongue slid from his mouth, and he looked at me with shocked eyes. "Is… is this true, Penelope?" he stammered.

"I think so, Boris," I said.

Boris stood up and walked to Granny, gazing down at the photograph in her lap. "Nanna Chang-Chang was a witch? Are you certain, Gladys? That's quite a thing to say if you're not totally sure of it."

Granny slid another photo from her apron pocket. "This picture is from my own photograph album," she said. "It was taken in the haven, not long before your grandmother died. That's me on the right — you won't recognise me, I got given my entry spell when I was in my early twenties."

In the haven, a witch was always the age at which he or she had been given their entry spell. I'd remain twenty-three whenever I entered the haven, even if I lived to be one-hundred. Many witches waited until they were close to death in the mortal world before moving to the haven permanently and gaining their immortality in a younger body.

"But Nanna looks so young in this photo. This

couldn't have been taken just before she died. She was almost seventy when she passed," said Boris.

"The photograph was taken in the haven, Boris. She's at the age when she was given her entry spell."

Boris looked up from the picture. "So she's alive? In the haven? Isn't that where witches go when they get old? So they don't have to die?"

"Most witches," said Granny, placing a hand between Boris's horns and rubbing his head. "Your grandmother was different though, Boris. In China, witches were considered devils. Chang-Chang probably brought that belief with her when she moved to Britain, and when your mother was born she would have done everything in her power to prevent your mother from knowing the truth. She didn't like being a witch, she didn't like the haven either, she chose to die in this world, and because she didn't help your mother develop her own magic skills, your mother would never have known that *she* was a witch either."

"And if she didn't know she was a witch, Boris," I said. "Then you wouldn't have known that…"

Boris looked at each of us in turn. "That I'm a witch," he whispered.

"Precisely," said Granny. "It makes so much sense, Boris. Fate sent you to my door, and you said yourself that you'd always believed in magic."

"I always have done," said Boris. "Since I was a little boy."

"That's because you are magic, Boris," said Granny. "And fate had everything planned out for you. Why do you think you came to me in the first place and ended up in the body of a goat? So you'd have to stay with me, that's why! Then your credit card just happened to expire, and we went to your house, where Penny recognised the photo of your grandmother."

All the talk of fate seemed very addictive, so I joined in. "Because I went looking for the clogs which belonged to your grandmother," I said. "The photo was above them. As if I was led to it."

"Why did you want the clogs, Boris," asked Willow. "What made you think of them?"

"I had a dream!" said Boris. "My grandmother was wearing them! She was telling me how they helped her posture. I woke up and thought of Gladys's back problems, and because you three were going to my house to collect the credit card, I asked Gladys to bring the clogs back too... and as you rightly say, Penelope, they led you to the photo of Nanna."

"You see?" said Granny.

Boris gasped. "Jumping Jehovah!" he said. "It is fate! But why? Why was I sent to you, Gladys? What does this mean?"

"I'm sure fate will let us know, Boris," said Granny, stroking the goats back. "We just have to be patient. The answer will come eventually."

CHAPTER FIFTEEN

he four of us stood in Bridge street. Barney stood on my left, and Willow and Susie stood to my right. We all looked up at the sign which ran the length of the the shopfront. The sign company had done a good job. Bright red lettering on a green background made the shop stand out, and even Mr Jarvis had popped out to have a look, convinced that our new shop would bring him additional business too. "I don't know much about witchcraft," he'd said, "but surely witches need vegetables for some spells? If they do, just send them next door to me. I'll give them a discount!"

Willow and I agreed, on the condition that if any of his customers complained about not being able to find love, or not being promoted in work, he'd send them to our shop for a spell or a potion.

Barney had lowered his voice when Mr Jarvis had gone back inside *The Firkin gherkin.* "You don't give people real spells do you?" he said. "I'm not sure how I'd feel about that. It could be dangerous. Or illegal."

Susie put his mind at rest. "I've known the Weaver family were witches since I was eleven," she said, "and in all that time they've never used magic for anything but the best of intentions."

I could have listed at least three-hundred times that Granny had used magic for less than good intentions, but I chose to keep quiet. Barney could discover the dynamics of the Weaver family is his own good time. I was in no hurry to expose the inner workings of a dysfunctional magical family to him.

The four of us stared at the sign. "What a fantastic name," said Barney. "Boris really hit the nail on the head when he came up with that."

Willow and I had asked everyone we knew to offer suggestions for the name. I'd wanted to name it after my floating shop of course, but *The Water Witch - Floating emporium of magic,* was hardly an apt name for a landlocked shop. At least the boat would remain named *The Water Witch.*

Granny's idea for the shop name had not even made it onto the shortlist. *Wicked witches of Wickford,* sounded more like a film, or a gang that Granny might have been a member of as a teenager — or an elderly woman, I supposed. Boris had really come up trumps though, and surprised us all when he'd suggested his idea.

"*The Spell Weavers — Emporium of magic*," read Barney. "I love it."

"It's really clever," agreed Susie. "And it looks so professional."

Barney placed his hat back on his head. "I'd love to stay a little longer, but duty calls. The fingerprint experts have lifted a partial print from Gerald Timkins's shotgun. They say the murderer wiped the gun, but not well enough."

"That's good news, isn't it?" I said.

Barney nodded. "It's not always simple, even with a print. We'll see if it matches Mrs Oliver's or Felix Round's prints which we took when we brought them in for questioning, if they don't match, which I'm assuming they won't, I'll run them through the system. If there's no match there, it'll be a question of finding the so called scarecrow man, or another suspect. It could take a while to solve the case."

"I'm sure you'll find out who did it, Barney," I said.

Barney looked at his feet. "I was going to ask a favour," he said, lifting his eyes.

"Yes?" I said. "I'll do anything I can for you."

"You know how you all helped me solve Sam Hedgewick's murder, using… magic?"

"You want us to use magic to solve this case for you, don't you, Barney?" said Willow.

"Something like that," muttered Barney. "If you can. Please. It would be a great help."

"It doesn't work like that," I said. "We can't just use magic to find out who committed a crime. We can help if you have a suspect, you know… with helping them open up a little."

"Making them talk, you mean. Like you did with Mrs Oliver," said Barney. "Can't you look in a crystal ball or something like that? You sell them in the shop, maybe you can find out who murdered Gerald using one of those? It's very important that this case is solved quickly."

"I'm afraid not, Barney," said Willow. "We'd love to help, we want to know who killed Gerald as much as you do, and we'll always be here for you, but you need to point us in the right direction before we can do anything. Why has it suddenly become so important, though? I mean — I know it's a murder and it needs solving, but why the sudden urgency?"

Barney sighed, and gave me a look I couldn't interpret. "No reason," he said, looking away. "And I'm sorry if I offended anyone by asking for magical help — I'm still coming to terms with what it means to find out that magic is real and… witches are real. I suppose I was hoping you'd be able to perform miracles."

"Not those sorts of miracles," I said, "but come to Mum's cottage tonight, and you'll see a different sort of miracle."

Barney raised an eyebrow. "Oh? What would that be?"

"She's going to the haven, Barney," said Willow. "And the miracle will be that all our family will be in one room, but the attention will be on Penny, not Granny or Mum."

"That *will* be a miracle, Barney," I said. "Believe me."

IT FELT odd allowing Barney to kiss me in front of my family, but even Granny looked happy that Barney and I were an item, and saved any sarcastic comments she may have had for another day.

Uncle Brian was dressed as stylishly as usual, although I was sure his choice of a blue crushed velvet suit would look better on the streets of Soho where he lived, than in Mum's country kitchen surrounded by four other witches, a magical goat, a journalist, and a very tall ginger policeman — still in his uniform.

Mum was wearing her best dress, and had obviously visited the hairdressers earlier in the day. Her hair looked freshly dyed, although everyone pretended not to know that most of the rich black was from a bottle. It was always tempting to point out grey hairs to her when they began appearing, but most people had learnt never to mention Mum's appearance to her unless it was a compliment.

Barney was a quick learner. "You look amazing, Maggie," he said, standing at my side. "Really lovely."

"Thank you, Barney!" gushed Mum. "You're a real gentleman. You look very smart too, I've always liked a man in uniform."

Barney left my side to speak to Boris and Granny, and Mum lowered her voice a notch or two. "I don't think that young man *is* of Scottish heritage after all," she said. "He's far too polite and well mannered. And I've yet to see him start a fight in a pub. I can admit when I'm wrong, and I *was* very wrong — there's less Scottish in Barney than there's sense in your grand-mother, and that's not a lot at all. I think he's perfect for you, Penelope."

Mum had been convinced that Barney was Scot-tish due to his red hair and the way he walked. We'd explained that Barney wasn't swaggering as Mum had suggested, he was simply uncomfortable because all his trousers were a little too short and dug into his nether regions. We didn't question Mum's unique view of the Scottish — she was a complicated woman — although she had alluded to the fact that Scottish witches had once caused a lot of trouble in the haven. She also believed that Shakespeare had been accurate and completely validated in his portrayal of Scottish witches in *Macbeth*.

"Thanks, Mum," I said. It was the nicest thing she'd said about any boy I'd ever dated. "We're taking it slowly, but I feel good about him. He's the same as me in so many ways."

"The way he acted the last time he was here sent him sky rocketing in your grandmothers estimation," said Mum. "There's not many mortals who would be so calm when confronted with magic. He was more concerned about you than the fact that your Uncle Brian had just magicked up a portal, and that we were talking about casting a spell on him. When you passed out, he was beside himself with worry."

I smiled. "I'm glad he knows we're all witches," I said. "It would have been hard to get close to him otherwise. It's not the sort of secret that's easy to hide from someone you're close to."

"Very true, Penny, and it's obvious you care for each other," said Mum. "That's the reason you got given your haven entry spell."

"The fact that I like Barney is responsible for me getting my spell?" I asked. "How does that work?"

Mum smiled. "No, the fact that you stuck up for him is the reason. That spell you cast to stop me hexing Barney was powerful magic. It was completely pure and was cast from a place of love. You put yourself at risk for the sake of Barney and proved that you're a good witch. That's why you got your spell."

Mum moved towards me, and I let her hug me. It was rare that she showed me any physical affection, and I settled into her arms with a sigh, enjoying her smell and each moment of closeness she allowed us.

"Are you ready to go to the haven?" she said, pulling herself from me. She turned away briefly, but I saw her wipe a tear from the corner of her eye.

"I'm ready, Mum," I said. "And I'm so proud and happy to be going with you on my first trip. It means a lot to me."

"Me too, sweetheart," said Mum. "I remember the day I first went to the haven. Your grandmother knitted me a lovely red pullover and bought me a new pair of shoes for the trip. It was the proudest day of my life. Until today of course — being able to accompany her own daughter to the haven for the first time is every mother's wish. Well, every *witch* mother's wish, I should say. Today is the proudest day of my life so far, and I'm sure I'll feel the same when Willow gets her spell too."

Barney arrived at my side and Boris trailed behind him. "Such exciting stories," said the goat. "You really have had a marvellous life, Barney."

"Thanks, Boris," said Barney. "I'll save the rest of

them for another time. Remind me to tell you about the time I took Mavis Henshaw down in the greengrocers shop. She was stealing lychees. Slipping them into her bag when Mr Jarvis wasn't watching. He saw her from out of the corner of his eye and called the police. They sent me, and it was quite the struggle, I can tell you."

I swallowed my laughter. I knew full well what had happened on that day. Eighty year old Mavis Henshaw had almost broken Barney's finger with her walking stick, forcing Barney to call for backup. I wouldn't make Barney look stupid in front of his new friend though.

"Barney's quite the hero," I said, drawing an approving nod from Boris.

The loud sound of smashing glass grabbed everyone's attention, making Mum spin on the spot and Boris jump with fright.

"What have you done?" said Mum. "That's one of my best crystal whisky glasses!"

Granny stared at the shattered glass at her feet, and put the spoon she was holding down on the table. "Sorry, Maggie. I was trying to get everyone's attention, like they do in the films. I only tapped it gently — either these glasses are not real crystal and you got seen coming a mile away, or I don't know my own strength! I'm sorry though, I suppose."

"It was an accident," said Mum, unusually diplomatically for her. "Don't worry about it. What did you want to say?"

Granny cleared her throat, and looked around the room, her gaze finally settling on me. I returned the gentle smile she gave me and let her speak.

"I wanted to say that I always knew Penny would grow into a wonderful young woman," she said, "and that I've been waiting for this day for a long time. It's a wonderful moment when a loved one steps through a portal into the haven for the first time. Today is a truly wonderful day."

"Hear! Hear!" said Boris, stamping his front hooves on the slate floor. "Well said, that woman!"

"Don't interrupt!" snapped Granny. "I haven't finished!" Granny put her arm around Brian's shoulder and pulled him close to her. "I'd also like to take this moment to congratulate my eldest child... my first born... my little gay angel... my beautiful Brian. A big round of applause for Brian please, everybody!"

"Stop it, Barney," hissed Mum.

Barney managed one more clap, and looked at me. "Don't clap," I urged, putting my hand on his.

Mum scowled at Granny. "What exactly are we congratulating Brian for, Mother?" she said. "This is Penny's special day!"

"Well," said Granny, "it's all very exciting! My big boy has decided that he's going to move from

London back to Wickford, and start a business as a hypnotist, here in town! Isn't that wonderful!"

"But he's not a hypnotist," said Willow. "He can't just practice as one. It's probably illegal. Isn't it, Barney?"

Barney shifted uncomfortably from foot to foot, no doubt refereeing a fight between his policeman's mind and the part of his brain that knew he should be terrified of confronting Granny. Luckily for Barney the sensible part won, and he kept quiet. He offered Willow an apologetic shrug.

Granny fixed her gaze on Willow. "Don't you dare tell Brian what he can and can't do, young lady," she said. "He's fought hammer and tongs to get where he is today. Do you think it's been easy for him to live in Soho as a gay man? Of course not, he's been oppressed at every turn, but here he is today, standing before us… loud and proud and more queer than ever!"

"It's not particularly hard living in Soho as a gay man, Mother," said Uncle Brian. "It's quite fun actually, and I can't recall being oppressed by anybody if I'm being perfectly honest with you. In fact, I've only ever been treated with respect."

"You've internalised the oppression, dear," said Granny, patting her son's hand. "It's quite normal. You've been oppressed so often that you've come to accept it as the norm, but it isn't, and you're a survivor, Brian!" Granny put her hands together. "A round of applause for my son please, everybody!"

"Stop clapping, Barney. I won't tell you again," snapped Mum. "That's enough of that for today, Mother. It's Penelope's day, and we've already wasted enough time. It's time for Penny to enter the haven!"

This time Mum allowed Barney to clap, and everybody else joined in too, including Granny.

"Just one thing," said Brian, "before the main event. What did you mean, Mother… when you said I was more queer than ever?"

"The suit, son," said Granny looking Brian up and down. "It's very, *very* camp. Crushed velvet should really only be seen on furniture, my darling."

"Really?" said Brian. "Is it camp?"

"A little," said Susie from her seat at the table. "But you do wear it well, Brian."

Mum slammed her glass down on a kitchen counter. "That's enough! It's time for Penny to open her portal." She put a gentle hand on my shoulder. "Go on, darling. Open your portal."

"I'm a little nervous," I said, standing closer to Barney. "I don't know why."

"I was the first time I stepped through my portal," said Mum. "But there's no need to be, honestly. You use the lounge doorway and I'll use the hallway doorway. You step through your portal first and then I'll step through mine. We'll appear close by one another in the haven, there's nothing to be scared of. I'll be with you every step of the way."

Barney held my hand. "It is safe, isn't it?"

Mum touched his shoulder to reassure him. "Barney, I know you don't know us very well yet, but you can be assured that nobody in this room would allow Penny to come to harm. We wouldn't let *anyone* in this room come to harm, and that includes you, young man. She's perfectly safe."

Susie got up from the table and stood next to Barney. "I've seen Maggie and Gladys open hundreds of portals," she said. "And I've never seen anything dangerous happen. She'll be fine, Barney."

I slipped my hand from Barney's, and stood on tiptoes to kiss him on his cheek. "I'll be okay." I promised. "Don't wait here for me though, I don't know how long I'll be away. I'll phone you when I'm back."

I stood before the lounge doorway, and Mum crossed the kitchen to the doorway which led into the hallway. Taking a final look around the room at the smiling faces, and Boris's yellow toothed grimace, I cast my spell.

The doorway creaked and quivered and filled with a bright shimmering light.

"Whoa!" said Barney. "That's amazing. It's beautiful. I can't believe what I'm seeing."

"I've seen it before," said Boris. "On Penny's boat. It's no better the second time."

"Very gold," said Uncle Brian. "Very you, Penelope."

"So, so," said Granny. "I've seen prettier portals."

"That's my girl," said Mum, opening her own portal.

"Go on, Penny, step through it," said Willow. "I want to hear all about it when you get back."

Taking a deep breath, I placed a foot over the threshold, shuddering as hairs stood on end and a breeze ran up my leg. I took one last glance at Barney, smiled at him, closed my eyes, and stepped into the light.

CHAPTER SIXTEEN

$\mathcal{E}$very muscle in my body tensed, and a loud whistling sound in my ears made me wince. A scary sensation of falling passed within a second, and I stumbled forward with my eyes closed and my arms held out to break my fall.

Somebody caught me almost immediately. "I've got you!"

"Mum," I said, opening my eyes and blinking. I shook my head a couple of times to rid my ears of the whistling, and stepped back from my mother. "Wow. You look… different!"

Mum looked at least twenty years younger, and the black of her hair was obviously not from a bottle. She was still overweight, but nowhere near as heavy as she'd been in her kitchen a couple of minutes before. She was younger than I was, I needed to remind myself. Mum had acquired her entry spell when she was twenty-one, and I was twenty three. It was unsettling having a mother who was younger than me, and it must have shown on my face.

"Oops, sorry!" said Mum. "I forgot to change."

In less time than it took to blink, Mum had transformed into the woman I knew, complete with recently dyed hair and a few extra pounds around her thighs and midriff.

"How?" I said. "I thought you always remained the age you were when you got your entry spell, when you're in the haven? That's what you've always told me and Willow."

"This is the haven, Penny," said Mum. "Anything's possible. We tell youngsters they'll always be the age they are when they get their spell so they'll work harder to acquire it. It worked for you didn't it? Every time you enter the haven, you'll be the age you were when you got your spell, but you can transform into any age you like when you're here, as long as it's between the age you were when you got your spell, and the age you are in the mortal world. There are plenty of witches here who don't want to look young again, they're happy in the body they have, but they'll never age if they stay in the haven, and if they want to be young again, even if it's just for a day, they can be. I prefer looking this age if I'm honest. I hated my body when I was younger, I was far too thin. I think I looked sickly. Your grand-mother didn't feed me enough — I was a hungry girl."

I stumbled and Mum grabbed me. "Are you okay?" she said.

I shook my head. "Not really. Coming through the portal wasn't as easy as I thought it was going to be," I said.

"You must have closed your eyes when you stepped through," said Mum. "I'm sorry. I forgot to tell you to keep them open, Penelope. Your brain can't cope with what's happening if your eyes are closed. Next time keep them open and it'll be a lot simpler."

I blinked again, and looked left and right.

"Close your portal," said Mum. "It's still open."

Sure enough, the familiar hum of an open portal throbbed behind me. I allowed the portal spell to slip from my mind and the sound stopped. "Where are we?" I said. "It smells damp."

Mum and I stood together in a stone archway. The moss covered stone walls were a few feet apart and the curve of the ceiling seemed low enough to touch if I jumped. It was like standing in a dark and dank soldier's sentry box.

"This is an entry arch," said Mum. "You use it to leave and enter the haven. Every town and village has a few of them, and the big cities have thousands."

"Cities?" I said. "There are cities here? In the haven?"

"Not cities as you know them," explained Mum. "There's no skyscrapers or busy roads, but thousands of people live in them, and there's lots to do. They're fun places to visit, but I wouldn't like to live in one. I prefer the peace and quiet of the countryside."

I'd regained my bearings, and couldn't wait to leave the damp arch I was standing in. "I want to see," I said, looking past Mum's shoulder at the light behind her.

Mum smiled. "Come on, I'll show you," she said. She took me by the hand and pulled me from the arch.

I squinted as Mum guided me into the bright light, and turned to look at the arch I'd come through. Five stone arches were built side by side in a row, and dim light still flickered in the two arches through which Mum and I had arrived.

I turned on the spot slowly as the sun warmed my face, and gasped as I took my first look at the haven. Mum slipped her arm through mine and squeezed my hand. "It's nice isn't it?"

"It's amazing," I said.

We stood on the peak of a grassy hill, and stretching before us in all directions, as far as the eye could see, was scenery so beautiful I wished I could climb inside it and wrap it around myself like a blanket — just looking at it wasn't enough. I wanted to be enveloped by it.

Butterflies danced in my stomach, and my ears and nose worked overtime to distinguish between smells and sounds as my eyes flitted from snow capped mountain top, to sparkling lake. The soft peach colour which lightly tinged the sky, painted the scenery in a gentle glow which brought the vivid green of the vegetation to life and gave the scenery a warmth which made me happy to be alive.

"'It's huge," I said.

"They say it's as big as the world we just left behind," said Mum. "But I wouldn't know how true that is. I tend to stay here in this area, where my friends and family live, but your grandmother has travelled extensively — and has probably caused trouble in every corner of the haven."

What about getting home?" I said. "How do I get back to the door in your kitchen?"

Mum pulled me closer to her. It was the longest that Mum had held me for as long as I could remember. "Whichever arch you use will open a portal to the last doorway you used to enter the haven through," she said, "unless you specifically think of somewhere else you want to go to, like Uncle Brian did when he appeared in my kitchen, but that's definitely not advisable. Wherever you go in the haven, Penny, even if you stay here for years and find yourself thousands of miles away from this spot — any of the archways you use will take you back to exactly where you came from. It's that simple."

I remained silent, appreciating the view, and enjoying feeling so emotionally attached to my mother. Birds soared high in the sky and a sheep bleated somewhere in the distance. The fragrant scent of wildflowers and grass was underlaid with the salty aroma of an ocean, but the only water I could see was in rivers and lakes. The haven was a welcome assault on my senses, and I smiled as a warm breeze blew a strand of hair from my eyes.

"Can you feel it?" said Mum. "I could when I first came here."

"Feel what?"

"The prickles," said Mum. "Like pins and needles on your skin."

I nodded. I could. "I thought it was a residual effect from the portal."

"The sensation will pass in minute or two, but what you're feeling is magic, Penny. *Real* magic, not like in the world we just left behind. When Maeve created the haven, she used almost all of the magic in the mortal world to create this dimension. The haven is how our world used to be before most of the magic was sucked from it. You'll find it a whole lot easier to cast spells here than it is in Wickford."

I shielded my eyes from the sun and studied the

valley below us. Smoke rose from chimneys on thatched roof cottages in a quaint village to our left, and a sprawling urban development was visible in the far distance.

"Look at the size of that forest." I said, squinting. "On the horizon. It's huge."

"It's a rainforest," said Mum, "like the Amazon Jungle."

"A jungle? In the haven?"

"Yes," said Mum with a smile. "This place is like the mortal world, Penny, but without the same rules. Here there might be a rainforest next to a desert, or a glacier next to a tropical beach. The haven creates the environments where witches lived in the mortal world, but not in the same geographic locations. Somewhere in the haven there's an ice cap where Inuit witches live."

Mum allowed me a few more minutes to soak up the atmosphere, before removing her arm from mine. "Come on," she said. "Aunt Eva can't wait to see you. She was going to meet us here, but she decided to cook you a welcome meal instead. She'll be waiting for us at her cottage."

THE WALK down the hill was nicer than any walk I'd taken at home. Rabbits hopped across the narrow path in front of us, and butterflies with vivid patterns flitted between wild flowers which grew from the lush green grass. Our surroundings were unspoiled, and I knew without asking that it would be perfectly safe to drink water from the little stream which bubbled and splashed down the slope alongside the path.

A fat dragonfly settled on my shoulder and I placed a finger in front of it as it spread it's wings to dry them in the breeze. It climbed onto my finger and I looked at Mum. "Aren't you nervous?" I asked. "There's a huge insect on my hand."

In the world we'd just left behind, Mum was terrified of insects, particularly insects which she considered capable of landing on any food she was about to eat. It was a serous condition, and one which had forced her to wear a bee-keepers hat when she'd visited my boat on the canal.

"I'm not nervous here," she said with a smile which lit up her face. "The haven has a way of making you feel calm... most of the time anyway." The dragonfly flew from my finger and Mum watched as it zig-zagged away. "This way," she said, leading us towards a stone bridge which spanned the stream where it widened into a river at the base of the hill.

Mum paused halfway across the bridge and called me alongside her as she leaned over the wall to look at the sparkling water below. "Look," she said. "You don't see trout like that in Wickford."

Long fat fish swayed rhythmically in the crystal clear water, inches below the surface. A fly broke the surface tension of the water above one of the trout, and the plump fish moved quickly, taking the fly before resuming its position in the current. "They taste good too," said Mum. "All food tastes good in the haven though."

I'd tasted food that Mum had brought home from the haven on many occasions in the past, and I was beginning to see why everything she brought back with her was so wholesome. It wasn't because of magic, as I'd thought — although some of the food she'd brought home in the past *had* been enhanced with magic — it was because the haven was unspoiled by mankind. The haven was how the world had once been, before humans began poisoning it with chemicals and clouding the atmosphere with pollution.

"How do you travel long distances?" I said, looking at the track we walked along. The ruts that were imprinted in the dirt surface looked like they'd been formed by the narrow wheels of a cart. "Are there cars here?"

"There's no cars," Mum said, "But there's steam trains and horses and carts. We have bikes too, and boats of course, and if you really wanted to be a little maverick, there's enough magic in the haven to fly a broom, although hardly anybody does — a broom is far too narrow to sit on. People have been injured very intimately while trying. I'm told that when one drunk male witch attempted to fly a broomstick, he hurt himself very badly when he flew into turbulence. I don't know who started the rumour that witches always fly around on broomsticks, but it certainly wasn't a witch, and definitely not a male witch — it was probably the same person who started the rumour that we have wart susceptible skin."

The dirt track we walked on gave way to cobblestones, and Mum hooked her arm through mine. "We're here," she said, as cottages with thatched roofs and neat gardens appeared around the bend. "Your home from home."

CHAPTER SEVENTEEN

*T*he little town was so painfully quaint it was as if Mum and I had stepped back in time, rather than through a magical portal — although for all I knew — we'd done both. My understanding of the haven had already been questioned by Mum's off the cuff admission that people could choose the age they were in the haven — it went against everything I'd ever been told about the place, but I supposed there was lots about the dimension that I was yet to learn, and lots that Mum had yet to tell me.

Cottages with thatched roofs lined the wider roads, and small shops were squashed tightly against one another in narrow lanes which were fragranced with the aroma of baking bread and pastries. People said hello as we made our way past the bustling town square, and I laughed as a small child in old fashioned clothing ran ahead of us with a hoop and stick. A toy I'd only ever seen in pictures.

"Why are there children here?" I asked. "Did they get their entry spells when they were really young? Were they really that good at magic?"

Mum guided us to the left and into an alley which led between two shops and brought us out in a park with a duckpond, a bandstand, and beds of vibrantly coloured flowers everywhere I looked. "People can have children here," said Mum. "The portal isn't like an x-ray machine — too much of it doesn't mess with a person's... special bits. Some of the children came here when the portal was first created, when Maeve conjured it up to stop witches being burnt at the stake. Some of the witches that fled here had children who they were allowed to bring with them, and those children will never grow up. They'll always be young if they don't leave the haven, and some of them don't want to — they remember the outside world as a cruel place which murdered people like them."

Two elderly men played chess on a board which was set up on the green painted bench between them, and both of them smoked long pipes. The shade of a large oak tree gave them protection from the warm sun, and they smiled as we neared them.

"Who's this, Maggie?" said one of them, removing his flat cap in a polite greeting. "Another one of the Weaver coven?"

"This is my eldest daughter, Herman," said Mum. "Her name's Penelope. This is her first time here."

The other man smiled. "Come here, Penelope," he said, peering at me through spectacles with lenses so thick they magnified his eyes to somewhere approaching the size of golf balls. "What's that behind your ear, young lady? Let me get it for you."

Mum sighed. "She's twenty-three, George, not five. She doesn't want to know what's behind her ear, and she's seen plenty of magic. No trick that you can do will be anything she hasn't seen before. You can't impress a witch with mediocre magic."

I giggled, and smiled at the old man. "Of course I want to know what's behind my ear," I said. "Go on, what's there? Get it for me."

I stood in front of George and bent at the waist as he reached for my ear. His calloused fingers brushed my face, and he laughed as the crackling sound of a spell being cast reverberated next to my head, and a glass full of black liquid with a white frothy head appeared in his hand.

"Oh! It's just a beer… for me," he laughed, his wrinkles tightening around his mouth. "Want a sip?" he asked, offering me the glass.

I pushed his hand away with a smile. "No thanks," I said. "If it had been elderberry wine, I might have said yes, but I have to be in certain mood for beer, especially when it's been behind my ear."

"You're just like your grandmother," said Herman, staring at me as he puffed on his pipe, the spicy pungent aroma of burning tobacco reminding me of my grandad. "You've got those mischievous eyes of hers. And the little smirk. Where is she anyway? I haven't seen Gladys for weeks and weeks. I miss her, and I'm sure she misses me just as much."

"She's taking a break from people like you, Herman," said Mum. "I can assure you she doesn't miss you."

George sipped his pint, and moved a chess piece on the board. "We heard she got witch dementia so she can't get through her portal, and that she turned three grown men into singing horses," he said. "Or donkeys. I don't remember which. Some species of farmyard animal anyway."

"Chinese whispers," said Mum, walking away. "It's nonsense, my mother's just staying away from the haven for a while." She smiled at me. "Come on, Penny, Aunt Eva's cottage is just around the next corner. She'll be wondering where we are."

"Goats!" said George. "That was it, she turned them into talking goats! That's what I was told!"

I laughed. One Boris was enough, three of them would have been a nightmare. "You've had too many of those beers," I said with a wink. "You're drunk."

"As witty as your grandmother too," said Herman, patting my hand. "Go on, get on your way. If your

Aunt Eva's waiting for you, you don't want to be late. She's worse than her sister."

"Worse than Granny?" I laughed, following Mum as she hurried off.

"Maybe not worse," shouted George. "But they're as bad as each other, that's for sure!"

"Ignore those old codgers," said Mum, as we left the park and turned right onto a long lane, the warm air fragranced by the sweet perfume of a large honeysuckle bush which grew in the small front yard of a cottage. "That's what happens if you don't try hard enough to get your entry spell when you're young. Those two men spent their lives in the mortal world drinking and playing cards, they were only given their spells because Maeve thought they'd die before they earned them the traditional way. Producing glasses of beer is about the only spell that George can manage, and they're stuck in those bodies however much they wish they were young again."

"I liked them," I said, watching a red squirrel bounding through the branches of the beech tree which spread its thick limbs across the road, offering us shade from the hot sun. "They reminded me of grandad."

Mum crossed the cobbled lane, and pointed at a beautifully maintained white cottage which was set back from the road and surrounded by colourful flowering bushes and leafy trees. "That's your Aunt Eva's home," she said. "She'll be thrilled to see you."

The crooked gate creaked as Mum pushed it open, and a fat bumblebee buzzed past my ear on its way to the apple tree which stood in the centre of the small lawn, heavy with bright red apples which begged to be picked.

The cottage door swung open, and Aunt Eva stood in the doorway, her apron covered in a light dusting of flour, and her smile as happy as her voice. "Penny!" she said, rushing down the path to meet me, pushing Mum aside without so much as a smile. "I've missed you! How you've grown — you were no higher than my waist when I last saw you!"

"Hi, Aunt Eva," I said, melting into her embrace. "You haven't changed a bit!"

Aunt Eva looked just as I remembered. No taller than Granny, but wider at the hips, and without the blue rinse perm. She was the older of the two sisters, but the reddish tint to the light in the haven took the age from her wrinkles. The folds of skin looked as soft as a peach.

"I made myself look this way just for you, darling," she said. "You don't want to see me as an nineteen year old just yet, it would be too much for you to take in." She released me from her hug, but kept her hands on my shoulders as she took a step backwards and looked me up and down. "You look just like Gladys did when she was your age," she said. "The resemblance is uncanny. You have her eyes."

I didn't know whether to take that as a compliment or an insult. In all the pictures I'd seen of Granny as a young woman, she'd always had the same glint in her eye — a glint which hovered midway between mischievous and evil. I was sure I didn't have the glint, but I *was* aware that when I was angry, people seemed to cower internally when I stared at them. Maybe I'd not fallen far from the tree where Granny was concerned. I smiled at Aunt Eva. "Thank you," I said, accepting it as a compliment.

Aunt Eva's mouth curled into a wide grin. "Come on, there's people waiting to meet you. I hope you're hungry. I do like baking, you see, and I got a little carried away with myself today. They'll be plenty of cakes for you to take home with you."

Aunt Eva's cottage smelt like the French patisserie which had recently opened in Wickford. The scents of cinnamon and vanilla vied with each other for my attention, and I licked my lips as I followed Mum and Aunt Eva into the large kitchen, where a long table was hidden beneath plates of cakes, scones, and breads.

"Wow," I said. "You baked all this today?"

Aunt Eva wiggled her fingers. "With a little help," she smiled. "I have a few spells which speed the process up. If you think the microwaves you have back in the other world are fast, you should see my pronto-pastry spell!" She picked up a tray laden with sandwiches, and passed it to me. "Would you be so kind as to carry this into the back garden please, Penelope? We're eating in the sun today."

Bright sunlight spilled through the kitchen window, and another realisation dawned on me. "It was evening when we left Wickford," I said, taking the tray from Aunt Eva. "Why is it still daytime here?"

Mum picked up a plate of scones and two pots, one brimming with cream and another full of jam. She balanced the pots on the edge of the plate and led the way out of the kitchen. "It's dark somewhere in the haven," she said. "We have time zones here too, they don't match perfectly with our world back home though. You get used to it the more you visit."

Aunt Eva pushed past us, carrying a large cake on a stand. "I can't wait to introduce you to my friends," she said. She lowered her voice as she pushed the back door open with a flick of her thigh. "Take whatever Hilda tells you with a pinch of salt, dear."

"Who's Hilda?" I said, following Mum and Aunt Eva into the sunlight.

"She's a seer," said Mum. "But she's very old. She came to the haven a long time ago, when Maeve first conjured it up. She was old when she got here, and she'd lost a few of her marbles already. Do as

Eva says, and take what she says with a *big* pinch of salt."

Mum and I followed Aunt Eva past the flower beds and bushes which teemed with bees and insects, and along the short pathway which snaked through a tiny orchard which was planted with two plum trees and three apple trees, all laden with fruit bigger and brighter than any I'd seen in a supermarket at home.

The scene beyond the orchard where wild grasses and flowers prevailed and a small fountain trickled water into the pond that surrounded it, reminded me of the Mafia films I'd enjoyed watching with Granny when she'd baby sat me as a young child. Mum had not been impressed at Granny's choice of entertainment for a five year old, but I had lovely memories of snuggling up to Granny on her sofa while one crime family slaughtered another on the television. Aunt Eva's guests looked like they'd be perfectly at home in the countryside of Sicily, and I smiled at the small group of people as Aunt Eva began her introductions.

Three people sat at the long wooden table, the legs protruding from grass and flowers, and the top already laid with plates, cutlery, and big wooden bowls of salad next to jugs of iced water. The whole scene screamed rustic Italian, and I placed the tray I was carrying on the table as I said my hellos.

At the head of the table, wearing a black knitted shawl which seemed overkill for such a lovely day, sat an elderly woman who peered at me with one eye. The other eye was covered with a bejewelled eyepatch which glinted in the light as she tilted her head to study me.

Next to her sat a muscular young man wearing a white shirt with the sleeves rolled up to his elbows, and the top three buttons undone. His blond hair glowed in the sun, and dimples gave a mischievous element to his smile as he greeted me. "Hello," he said, his voice as soft as the butter which was melting on a little plate in front of him. "I'm Gideon. Gideon Sax."

He stood to shake my hand and I gazed up at his handsome face, knowing right away that Willow would be infatuated with him. "Hi," I said. "I'm Penelope."

He chuckled. "We know who you are," he said, releasing my hand. He indicated the elderly woman at the head of the table with a nod. "This is Hilda Truckle," he said, "and the old rogue opposite me is Alfred Stern."

I said my hellos and sat down to the right of Gideon in the chair he politely pulled out for me.

Hilda remained quiet, studying me with one eye, as Aunt Eva and Mum took a seat each. Mum sat to my right and Aunt Eva sat next to Alfred who poured me a glass of water and passed it across the table. "Gideon calls me an old rogue," smiled Alfred, his old eyes still managing to sparkle with young joy. "But would you believe me if I told you he was two-hundred years older than me?"

"One-hundred-and-ninety-three to be precise," said Gideon, nudging me playfully with an elbow. "That's how many years I came to the haven before you did. And you are rogue, Alfred. You were a highway robber in the other world, before you got too old to ride a horse. There's nothing more roguish than a highway robber. Especially one who used magic to commit his crimes."

"A rogue I may be," said Alfred, offering me a conspiratorial wink, "but I never hurt anyone, and I was better at highway robbery than you were at piracy."

"You were a pirate?" I said, glancing at Gideon. "A real pirate?"

"Aye," said Gideon. "That I was. I was caught though, when I was twenty-four. They were going to hang me, and I hadn't developed enough magic skills to stop them. The walk to the gallows is a long one, let me tell you."

"How did you escape the hangman?" I said.

Gideon laughed. "I'd done no real evil as a pirate, I enjoyed the women and rum, and the loot of course, but like Alfred, I'd never hurt anyone — so Maeve granted me my entry spell — a little late for my liking, but I like to think I left that world in style."

"How did you leave that world?" I said.

Gideon gave a sly grin, and closed his eyes for a moment. "As they were placing the hood over my head and preparing the noose, Maeve granted me my spell. The only doorway I could use was the trapdoor they were about to drop me through. It was still open after the unfortunate soul before me had passed through it — on the end of a rope — to whatever place waited for him. I cast my spell and a portal opened. I took a single step forward and shouted 'farewell cruel world' as I dropped. It was quite the show, I'm sure — it *must* have been — although I was very disappointed to be told I never made it into your history books."

"Enough!"

The piercing shout from the head of the table made Alfred jump, and I did well not to spill my glass of water.

Aunt Eva put a theatrical hand over her chest. "Hilda!" she said. "You darn near gave me heart attack! Could you show some manners and let us know when you're going to shout like that? What will Penelope think? You haven't even said hello to her yet."

"I've seen," said Hilda, her eye rolling in its socket as she studied my face. "I've seen."

"What have you seen?" said Mum, touching my arm briefly in what I assumed was an attempt to reassure me. "Have you seen another jumbled vision? Don't you go filling my daughter's head with your nonsense now, Hilda."

Hilda lifted a trembling hand and pointed at me. "You hold the heart of a lawman!" she said, her voice quivering. "A tall lawman with hair like the very fires of hell. Tell me it's so!"

"Let the girl eat, Hilda," said Aunt Eva. "You can read her fortune later."

"It's okay," I said. "I want to know what she means. She's talking about Barney."

Aunt Eva shrugged, and Gideon bit into a chunk of ham.

I smiled at Hilda. "Yes," I said. "It is so. Although his hair's more like a ginger bird nest, than the very fires of hell."

Hilda's finger remained where it was, pointing at my face. She spoke slowly. "The lawman will be gone from your life. Taken from you by malevolent forces while he's still young and virile! Such a shame, but it will be so! It will be so! I have seen and I have spoken!" Her eye widened, and she lowered her arm. She pointed to the small yellow dish in front of me. "Pass me the olives would you? I like the black ones."

CHAPTER EIGHTEEN

"*H*ilda!" said Aunt Eva. "You can't just tell Penelope that the man she's involved with is going to die, and then ask for the olives. Have some etiquette would you — at least tell her *how* he's going to die. I don't know — you seers, you're all about *you*."

I understood what George and Herman had meant when they'd said that Granny and Aunt Eva were as bad as each other. Neither of the sisters had an ounce of tact.

Mum put a hand on my shoulder and Gideon put his hand over mine. "What do you mean, Hilda?" I said, aware of the shaking in my voice and the cold finger that touched my spine. "What's going to happen to Barney?"

Impatient of waiting for me to pass her the olives,

Hilda popped a sun dried tomato in her mouth and took a sip of water. She chewed as she looked at me thoughtfully. "I did *not* say he was going to die." She looked at the elderly man to her left. "Did I, Alfred? You've got your head screwed on right and your ears clear of wax — did I *once* say that anyone was going to die?"

Alfred buttered a piece of crusty bread. "You did imply it, Hilda. We've warned you about it in the past, and you keep promising that you're not doing it for theatrical effect, but I have to admit, Hilda... I really think you take pleasure from scaring people."

Gideon, Mum, and Aunt Eva mumbled their agreement.

"Tish-tosh!" snapped Hilda. "I say it as it comes to me. I *see*, you see? My visions must be delivered to their rightful owners, and the last one was for Penelope. I make no apologies for my style of delivery." She lifted her eye patch and gazed around the table with both eyes. "Where's the soft cheese? I don't see it."

Aunt Eva saw me staring at Hilda. "It's a style statement," she said, shrugging. "Those stones she's used to decorate it with aren't real diamonds either — they're as fake as most of her prophecies, I wouldn't take any notice of what she says."

I moved my stare from Hilda to Aunt Eva. "I wasn't looking at her because she's wearing an eyepatch she doesn't need," I said. "I'm staring at her because I want to know what she means about Barney! For goddess's sake — will someone please tell me what she means about Barney?" A warm tear spilled onto my cheek, and I looked at Hilda again. "Please," I said. "What did you mean, Hilda? I have to know. I feel sick."

"Honey baked ham?" said aunt Eva, pushing a plate of sliced meat over the table at me. "It goes wonderfully well on the rye bread, and it'll take the sickness away. The ham itself comes from a part of the haven where they really know how to breed good meat, and the honey's from a delightful woman who lives not a mile from here. Her bees are as fat and healthy as a chubby baby."

My eye twitched. "I *do not* want fat baby bee honey ham. I *do not* want to hear one more word from anyone, unless it's to tell me what the heck is going to happen to Barney! Hilda, I'll ask you one more time — what did you see?"

Hilda swallowed what was in her mouth, replaced her eyepatch, and sat back in her chair. Gideon and Alfred pretended to be more interested in the food which was on their plates, than the tension which was rising with each second that Hilda kept the information she had about about Barney from me.

I fixed Hilda with a stare which I imagined resembled Granny's sternest scowl. "Go on."

Hilda cleared her throat. "The lawman isn't going to die. Not yet anyway, but I can see with hindsight how you may have misconstrued the meaning of what I said. But that's on you, not me. I can't help what images you attach to the simple words I speak."

"Hilda," warned Mum. "Tell the girl. I want to know too, I've got quite the soft spot for Barney now I know he's not Scottish."

Hilda spoke slowly. "He will be taken away from you by the people who tell him what to do — his superiors. If he doesn't solve the terrible crime he's investigating — a murder, I see. The fiery haired lawman will be sent to a distant land, far from you and your love for him." She popped an olive into her mouth from the bowl I slid towards her. "A green and pleasant land with mountains which touch the sky and people who speak in riddles."

"What are you talking about?" said Mum. "What land? Barney lives in England, not a fantasy novel setting."

Hilda furrowed her frown and concentrated. "The land is known as Wales, and it will be the new home of the lawman if he doesn't complete his quest. He hides this knowledge from you."

"Barney will move to Wales if he doesn't solve the murder he's investigating?" I said. "Because his superiors will tell him to, and he knows about this, but has kept it secret from me? Is that what you're trying to tell me?"

Hilda nodded. "That's about the crux of it, I suppose. The messages come in pictures and I do my best to translate them into words you will understand."

Aunt Eva slid another plate across the table. "Hard boiled egg, Penny? They go very well with the spicy chorizo dip."

I took one out of politeness not hunger, and thanked Gideon as he passed me a fork. Alfred reached for the ham, and Hilda gave me a wry smile.

"I don't understand why Barney will have to leave if he doesn't solve a crime," I said, looking at Hilda. "That makes no sense."

"I can only tell you what I see," said Hilda between chews.

"Can you help Barney solve the murder?" I asked. "Can you see anything which will make his job easier?"

Hilda shook her head. "I can't see the past, only the present and the future. The past is a wall of impenetrable fog, which no seer can penetrate."

"Can you tell me anything that will help?" I said. "Please try."

Hilda stared at me for a few moments. "Give me your hand, witch."

Gideon sat back in his seat as I offered Hilda my

hand, which she took in hers. Her fingers closed on me with more strength than her thin body suggested she'd possess, and a faint electric current seemed to pass between us as she closed her eye and concentrated.

Hilda's eye opened suddenly, and she squeezed my hand. "You seek a man!" she said. "A man who makes men of straw!"

"Yes! A scarecrow man! Can you tell me who it is?" I urged. "Can you tell me his name? What is the name of the man who makes scarecrows?"

Hilda mumbled incoherently and dipped her chin. "I can't see. The image is murky, but — wait!"

"Yes?"

"I see a horned man with cloven feet who can help you!" said Hilda. She stared at me with a nervous eye. "Who are you that the lord of darkness himself would help you? Who are you that he who has many names would help you? Who are you that Beelzebub himself, master of demons and lover of fire would speak to you with news of the scarecrow man?" I gasped as Hilda snatched her hand from mine. Her voice trembled and she took a deep breath. "Who are you, friend of the cloven footed bringer of doom?"

I sighed. "Erm… could it be a man who's been turned into a goat you're talking about?" I said.

Hilda tilted her head as she considered. She

nodded sagely. "That makes so much sense," she said. "That would explain why the devil in my vision was white and didn't have a thrice pronged fork. Does this goat man have a grin of teeth most yellow?"

I nodded. "They are very yellow, yes."

"Then you must ask the goat man what he knows. He harbours information, and what he knows will guide the lawman to the man he so urgently seeks."

"Boris — the goat man, knows who the scarecrow man is?" I said.

"Harfa bell!" yelled Hilda, startling the birds from the trees. "Ask him of harfa bell!"

"Half a bell?" said Gideon. "Is that what you're saying, Hilda?"

Hilda shrugged. "Harfa bell — half a bell. I can't be sure which. Penelope must ask the goat man, and he will reveal his knowledge." Hilda reached over the table. "Give me your hand one more time, young witch."

I did as she asked, and Hilda concentrated as she squeezed my fingers. She muttered something under her breath and released her grip on me. "You're more than you think you are, Penelope Weaver," she announced. "The goddess has seen fit to bcstow upon you a gift which will reveal itself to you when the time is right."

"Gift?" said Mum, spooning cream onto the big dollop of jam which crowned the scone on her plate.

"What gift, Hilda? Penelope's never show any signs of been gifted."

"Thank you," I breathed. "It's lovely to know my mother thinks I'm not gifted."

"You know what I mean," said Mum. "Don't be so tetchy, young lady. Hilda's told you that Barney's going to be okay. Bring it down a notch or two would you?"

"Hilda's told me that Barney knows he may have to leave Wickford, and he's hidden it from me while at the same time beginning a relationship with me. I think I can afford to be a little *tetchy*, Mother."

Mum snorted. "That's men for you. Always keeping important secrets to themselves. Get used to it, or stay single — that's my advice."

Birds had begun returning to the trees since Hilda had stopped yelling, and Aunt Eva tossed a piece of bread to a brave one which flew to the ground and pecked around for scraps of food near the table. "That's enough arguing for today," she said, looking between me, Mum, and Hilda. "Penelope — I'm sure things will work out with this Barney gentleman you've met. Maggie — your daughter is bound to be upset by her boyfriend keeping secrets form her, and Hilda — what gift does Penny possess? Please tell me it's the gift of alchemy."

"It's a gift far greater than that of alchemy," said Hilda, with a sparkle in her eye. "She is a witch of the highest calibre, a witch born to lead, a witch who will touch people's lives in positive ways and who will be held up as an example of greatness in every land she steps foot in. She is a force to be reckoned with."

"Oh, no," said Mum. "She's a bloody seer isn't she? That's all I need — a prophet in the family. I've got enough problems with my mother, without adding a jumped up fortune teller to the mix."

Hilda took my hand again. "You are indeed a seer, Penelope. The gift will make itself shown when you need it most. Use it wisely and do no ill with it, for it is a gift of great power, to be sure."

Mum tutted. "Great power. More like trouble with a capital t."

"I'm a seer?" I said. "I'll be able to see into the future?"

Hilda nodded. "Indeed, Penelope Weaver. You will."

A cherry tomato bounced off my nose and Alfred laughed. "You didn't see that coming, did you?" he chortled. "You can't see very far into the future at all."

"She will, Alfred," said Hilda, arming herself with an olive which she tossed in the cheerful man's direction. "Just give the gift time to make itself shown."

Alfred's cheeky smile and mischievous demeanour broke the tension which was building, and after a few barrages of olives and tomatoes from everyone around the table, including Mum who even managed a full belly laugh as an olive she threw bounced off Gideon's forehead, we all settled down again.

"I don't mean to be rude," I said, "I know you made this meal to welcome me, Aunt Eva, but I really think I should get home now. I need to speak to Barney."

"And ask the goat man for his information," added Hilda.

Aunt Eva stood up. "Make sure to come back soon, Penelope. It was lovely seeing you, and remember to take some food back with you. I'll plate some cakes and scones for you. Willow will enjoy them."

"Not this time," said Mum. "I don't like the idea of carrying plates back up the hill to the portal arches."

"You're not going to make the poor girl use the arches are you?" said Hilda. "I told you, she's a talented witch. She'll be able to use a doorway in Eva's cottage. She's more than capable. I've seen it."

"Use a doorway in Aunt Eva's cottage?" I said, turning to Mum. "You told me I had to use one of the arches we arrived through."

"That's what they tell newcomers," said Gideon. "It's safer to use an arch they say, but I wouldn't know. I've never left the haven since the day I arrived, this place is much nicer than the world I left behind. A little more mad at times, but nicer."

"Penny can't use a doorway in the cottage," said Mum. "I won't let her risk it. She's not experienced enough. She could end up anywhere."

"Give the girl a chance," said Alfred. "She seems as bright as a button to me. I'm sure she'll manage it without a problem."

"Yes," I said. "Give me a chance. It can't be that hard."

Aunt Eva smiled. "It's not hard, sweetheart, come on inside with me, and I'll explain how to do it."

"Be it on your head, Eva," said Mum. "If she ends up in Australia, you can pay for her airfare home."

"It won't come to that," said Aunt Eva, leading the way back through the orchard. "And if she does end up in Australia she can open another portal which will bring her back here."

Hilda, Gideon, and Alfred followed us into the cottage, and we all stood in the kitchen together as Aunt Eva explained how to open a portal in Mum's kitchen back home. "You need to picture the room you want the portal to open in," she said, "really focus on it. Smell the familiar smells and picture the colour of the walls, and when you're ready, cast your spell. The portal that opens here will take you straight home, and if it doesn't, just open one wherever you end up and step back through, you'll find yourself in one of the arches at the top of the hill. There's nothing to worry about, your mother's over concerned."

Mum sighed. "I'm not *over* concerned, Eva, just concerned." She put her hand on my shoulder as I stood in front of Aunt Eva's kitchen doorway, holding a tray of goodies and ready to open my portal. "Penelope, I try and focus on three permanently placed things in the kitchen, it really helps to stabilise the spell. I use the Lionel Richie clock above the door, the magnet on the fridge which your grandmother brought back from Cuba, and the aga stove. Can you see those things clearly in your mind?"

Lionel Richie was Mums's favourite singer and one time crush. It was no problem to envision the Lionel Richie clock. The singer's cheesy grin and perfect hair had haunted me since I was old enough to tell the time. The internal mechanics had stopped working long ago, but Mum kept the clock hands showing the time as half past six, so they didn't interfere with Lionel's good looks.

The aga stove was similarly easy to picture, and the fridge magnet depicting Fidel Castro beneath a halo was an easily remembered bone of contention in the household, but an item which Granny insisted stayed where it was under threat of a curse on the person who dared to remove it.

Granny had given up on her plans to move to Cuba one day, and when her cat, Che Guevara had died, she'd finally agreed to discontinue her habit of wearing an ill-fitting beret whenever she attended protests.

I pictured the three items in my mind and looked at Mum. "I'm ready," I said.

Aunt Eva kissed me on the cheek, and Hilda, Gideon, and Alfred said their goodbyes as I cast my spell and the doorway flooded with shimmering gold.

With a final warning from Mum to be sure to open another portal immediately if I didn't end up in her kitchen, I stepped through the doorway, this time with my eyes open.

I stepped out of the other side with far more dignity and balance than when I'd taken my first portal journey, and for the first time in my life was happy to see Lionel Richie gazing down at me. Nobody was waiting for me in the kitchen, and I shut my portal.

No sooner had I closed mine than Mum's opened in the same doorway, and she stepped through with a look of relief on her face when she saw I was safe.

"I knew you could do it," she said, placing the tray she'd brought with her on the table. "I had every confidence in you."

"That's so good to hear," I said, hoping the sarcasm was evident in my voice. "It's lovely to know that your mother has confidence in you."

I placed the tray I'd brought with me next to Mum's and saw the note on the table.

Penny — Barney's been called into work — forensics have found something interesting on Gerald Timkins's shotgun. Me and Susie have gone back to the boat. I had a phone call from the delivery man — my new bed's arrived — so me and Susie are going to move it aboard.

Can't wait to hear all about the haven.

See you soon,

Willow x

P.S. Remember it's the pie eating competition tomorrow. I thought we could go in the boat as it's taking place so close to the canal.

P.P.S Boris and Granny want to come with us on the boat. I said that would be lovely. (I didn't mean it, but I wanted to be a little more like you, and show some manners.)

CHAPTER NINETEEN

J'd got back to the boat late at night and spent an hour telling Susie and Willow all about my trip to the haven. Susie had seemed jealous that I had such a beautiful place to visit whenever I wanted to, and Willow was excited about gaining her own entry spell — promising herself, me, and Susie, that she was going to practice her magic every day in an attempt to gain her spell as soon as possible.

The next morning, Willow and I shared breakfast on the picnic bench next to the boat, tossing Mabel and Rosie scraps of bacon and sausage as they begged at our feet.

It was going to be a busy day. Barney was on his way to the boat to find out what Hilda had meant about Boris knowing something about the scarecrow man. Barney, Willow, and I were going to visit Boris ourselves to find out what he knew — Barney had been sensible enough not to tell his superiors that he was going to be interviewing a goat — he'd say the information had come from elsewhere if Boris did prove to be helpful.

With the pie eating contest in the afternoon, we had a full day lined up.

I hadn't mentioned anything to Barney when I'd spoken to him on the phone about everything else Hilda had said. I wanted to ask him to his face if he was hiding anything from me. I knew our relationship was still young, but if there'd been a possibility that *I* was going to be moving away, I would have told Barney before taking the next step in our relationship. Maybe that was the traditionalist streak in me, but I thought I was well within my rights to question Barney on something he was evidently hiding from me. Something that might affect me as much as him.

Susie had told me and Willow that the police had questioned Sandra Timkins again, and she'd confirmed what Mrs Oliver had said — Gerald *had* had a disagreement with a man, but Sandra didn't know who he was, or what the argument had been about — only that it concerned the new crow scaring devices Gerald had bought to take the place of his scarecrows. She'd considered it so minor an altercation that she'd forgotten about it until the police had jogged her memory.

Willow squirted ketchup onto the sausage sandwich she'd made. "I'd have thought you'd have been more excited about finding out you're going to be a seer some day," she said. "I know I would. Imagine the possibilities that could come from being able to see the future."

I smiled. "If you'd seen Hilda, you'd understand. If all seers end up as batty as her I rather hope my gift doesn't make itself known to me for a long time to come. Preferably never."

"If she's that batty, why do you think she's right about Barney? Maybe she's mixed up."

I shook my head. "No. I believe her. I'm not saying she's wrong about what she sees, just that she's batty in the way she explains it to people. Imagine what Granny would be like if she could see the future and you'll have some idea of what Hilda's like."

Willow bit into her sandwich and nodded towards the pathway which led from the hotel. "Barney's here," she said.

"Would you think it was rude if I took him aboard *The Water Witch* to speak to him about it?" I said.

"Of course not!" said Willow. She pointed at my plate. "Does that mean I can have your bacon?"

I stood up, laughing. "Help yourself," I said. "I'm still full from all those cakes we ate last night."

Willow, Susie, and I, had devoured the baked

treats I'd taken back to the boat, but I'd had the presence of mind to save a few cakes for Barney. He could have them if it transpired he'd not been hiding something from me. Who was I kidding? He could have them even if he *had* — Aunt Eva's baking was far too tasty to keep from anybody — even a boyfriend who'd been obtrusive with the truth.

Barney said hello to Willow as he followed me onto the boat. We entered using the bow decking doors and Barney ducked low as we stepped down into Willow's bedroom.

Willow's new bed was in place, and she'd begun painting the walls a calming duck egg blue. It was surprisingly upsetting to smell fresh paint as I entered the room in which the shop had once been — instead of smelling herbs and incense — but I reminded myself that not more than two hundred yards away was the shop which Willow and I owned. The grand opening was scheduled for the beginning of the forthcoming week, although grand was perhaps not a word we should have been using to describe a gathering of less people than could be counted on two hands.

Barney followed me through the boat to the living area, keeping his head low. "I thought we were going straight to your grandmother's to speak to Boris," he said as he took a seat at the dinette table. "It's urgent we speak to him a soon as possible. We need to find out who the scarecrow man is."

"Just how urgent, Barney?" I said, sitting down next to him and staring out of the window at Willow, who was overfeeding the two animals who had her wrapped around their figurative little fingers.

Barney put his hat on the table and placed his radio next to it. "There's a murderer to be caught. I think that's pretty urgent," he said.

"I'll get to the point," I said, not wanting to waste time. Finding out who'd killed Gerald was more important than my feelings, but I needed some sort of answer before carrying on with the rest of the day. "I told you what Hilda said about Boris, but that wasn't all she said. She also told me something about you."

I studied his face for clues, but his expression was as friendly and open as ever. I resisted the urge to wipe the dried toothpaste from his chin and waited for him to answer.

"What about me?" he said. "Something good I hope."

"Barney, are you hiding something from me? Something about you *really* needing to solve this crime — like, if you *don't* solve it, you'll have to go and live in Wales. That sort of thing."

Barney's eyes narrowed. "Wow. Hilda knew about that? She really is talented."

"So?" I said. "It's true? Don't you think you should have told me before I let you kiss me in the restaurant? I wouldn't have been so keen to start a relationship with you if I knew you might be moving away from here. I'm not sold on the whole idea of long distance relationships."

"I didn't know then," said Barney. "I only found out yesterday morning. I didn't tell you because I didn't want you worrying about me, and anyway, Hilda's not entirely correct — I won't be going to live in Wales whatever happens. It was just an option, and it's not just me who's being pressured to solve the crime — it's all of the Wickford police."

"Tell me," I said. "I don't understand."

Barney sighed. "Wickford's a small town. It hardly needs a police station of its own — a larger one in Covenhill could cover most of the county, and that's what the moneymen want, but they need us to mess up before they can get their way. They want us to fail at solving Gerald Timkins's murder so they can make us admit failure and accept outside help."

"They want to prove the Wickford police are not fit for purpose?" I said.

"Something like that," said Barney. "They want everything centralised these days, but they need a good reason to implement their plans. A failed murder investigation is the perfect excuse."

"But where does Wales fit into this? Why would you need to move away?"

"If they close down the station in Wickford, those of us who still have years left to serve could either resign from the police or agree to being posted else-where. They can't just sack us."

I understood. "So they'll tell you to either accept a position in Wales or resign?"

Barney nodded. "Yup," he said, "but I won't move away whatever the outcome. I love my job, but I'm loving getting to know you even more, and your family — mad as they might be. I couldn't imagine having to go and live hundreds of miles away from you."

"You'd leave your job for me?" I said, taking his hand in mine. "That's a lovely thing to say, but I'd never want you to do that. You enjoy being a policeman too much. I couldn't live with the knowl-edge that you gave it up for me."

Barney put his hat on and grabbed his radio. "So what are we waiting for? I've got a crime to solve. I need to show that the Wickford police are worth keeping — come on, I've got a goat to interview, and I need your help."

I followed Barney through the boat and climbed ashore with him. Willow joined us as we headed up the footpath to the hotel where Barney had parked the car, and Rosie and Mabel wandered off to bully a family of brave swans who'd made the mistake of considering the patch of grass next to the boat as being a good place to relax.

We could still hear Mabel barking as we got into

the police car, and a scrap of paper on the dash-board reminded me of the note Willow had left for me at Mum's cottage. The note had said that the forensics department had discovered something on Gerald Timkins's shotgun, but with all the excited questions coming from my sister and Susie about my trip to the haven, it had slipped my mind the night before.

"They found a microscopic piece of dried paint," explained Barney when I asked. He took a right onto Church street, and an immediate left into the lane which would take us to Ashwood cottage. "Green paint, on the trigger guard, but it's so small it will take them some time to work out exactly what paint it is. Mrs Timkins said Gerald was always painting too, and his tractor's green — so there's a good chance it came off that. It's something and nothing, but it needs to be investigated."

Barney took the right turn onto Granny's property and parked next to the lean-to. He looked at the cottage and gave a little shudder as he laughed.

"What's so funny?" said Willow.

Barney looked up at the guest bedroom window. "I'm remembering the last time I was here, thanks to the memories Penny gave back to me. I'm still coming to terms with the fact that there's a man's body in the bedroom who's mind is in a goat. It's like a dream, and to think that for all the years I've known your family… you've been witches. It's hard to get my head around."

I'd tried to put myself in Barney's position. I thought I could empathise with him, but I'd never truly know what it would feel like to discover that magic and witches existed after spending my whole life thinking they were mere fantasy. Magic had always been a part of my life. My earliest memory was of Mum opening a portal in the kitchen doorway, and some of my best memories involved magic of some kind. Barney was doing really well to take it all in his stride so easily.

"Come on," I said, opening the car door. "This time it'll be easier. There's no secrets anymore."

"Where are they?" said Willow. "We told Granny we were coming, but the Range Rover's not here."

The roar of an engine from the woodland behind the cottage gave us a clue, and I took my phone from my pocket. Granny answered on the third ring, and after boasting she was speaking to me using the cars bluetooth technology, as if it were more special than magic, she told me where she was and that she'd be back at the cottage promptly.

"They're off-roading," I explained, slipping the phone into my pocket. "I could hear Boris screaming, so I don't think Granny's very good at it."

"Or too good," suggested Willow.

The sound of the engine grew louder until the

Range Rover appeared at the end of one of the narrow trails which led into the woodland that spread for miles behind Granny's cottage. It's black paintwork was splattered with mud, although the private registration plate was still visible. It read B1TC HY, and never had a registration plate been more fitting for the person who drove the vehicle.

Barney and Willow jumped backwards as Granny skidded to a halt in front of us, and I held a hand up to protect my face from the gravel which the tyres spat at us.

Granny gave us a wave before climbing from the vehicle and rushing around to the front passenger door. "Quick! Help me get him out. The carpet in this car cost more than all the carpets in my cottage put together, and I do not want sick on it!"

Boris had obviously been using the door for support, and he thudded to the gravel as Granny opened it and he fell out of the vehicle.

"It's all okay," said Granny. "He wasn't sick. Well done, Boris."

Boris groaned and got to his feet, he took a step forward and Barney caught him before he slipped and fell again. "Careful, Boris," he said. "Get your balance before you try again."

"I begged you to slow down, Gladys," murmured Boris, his eyes closed as he wobbled on his four legs. "I begged you."

Granny slammed the door shut and took the large sunglasses from her face and replaced them with her regular purple spectacles which she took from a pocket.

"What are you wearing, Granny?" said Willow. "I think I preferred it when you wore an apron everywhere you went."

"I told you before, sweetheart," said Granny, sauntering past Boris, who dribbled from his mouth and took a deep breath. "I'm in a different class now. I need to look the part."

"You look like a posh farmer," said Willow.

Granny's waxed jacket and expensive wellington boots over tweed trousers certainly gave the impression that she was a wealthy landowner, but the insistence in keeping her blue perm kept the top fifth of her body firmly grounded in the working class.

"Thank you, darling," said Granny. "I appreciate the compliment."

"Don't worry, Gladys," said Boris, regaining his balance. "I'm fine. Don't you worry about me. I'll just stand here with my stomach in knots as a result of your atrocious driving."

"Quiet! Know your place!" snapped Granny. "Don't you dare speak to me in such tones! Take the Range Rover away and clean it. I want to be able to see my face in it when you've finished, and when you've done that, you can water the horses and bring me my drink — a Gibson cocktail, and don't you dare forget the onion this time or I'll have your job, and then who'll put food in the bellies of that fat family you insist on keeping? I'll make sure you never work for the landed gentry again! You'll be down the mines before you can say 'please, Lady Weaver, I won't do it again — I suggest you think on that."

"Not in front of them, Gladys," said Boris. "I told you I'd play along, but only in private."

"Ooh. I got carried away. Sorry, Boris," said Granny. She looked at our puzzled faces. "Boris and I like to play aristocrat and commoner," she explained. "It's just a little fun. We enjoy role playing."

"Is that how you think the aristocracy speaks to their employees?" said Willow, following Granny into the cottage.

"I certainly hope they do," said Granny. "Otherwise what's the point of privilege? Anyway, enough of that depressing talk— you came here to speak to Jeeves, erm — I mean, Boris, didn't you? Come on in, I'll put the kettle on."

CHAPTER TWENTY

*W*ith her waxed jacket and wellington boots removed, Granny looked half normal again, and when she slipped her apron on as she served us tea, she was completely herself once more.

"How can I help?" said Boris, fully recovered from his car sickness, and with the remains of a saucerful of brandy around his lips. "Gladys says I was mentioned during your trip to the haven, Penelope?"

"A seer told me you may be able to help us find the man the police want to speak to about Gerald Timkins's murder," I said.

Granny sat in her favourite seat near the unlit fire, and Boris stood next to her. The paintings of family ancestors looked down at us from their places on the walls, and Barney seemed to wilt under their oil painted gazes. I didn't blame him — some of my ancestors looked like the type of people you wouldn't like to meet in a well lit high street, let alone a dark alley.

Boris looked at me with interest. "Me? I may have information which will help apprehend a murderer?"

"Murder suspect," said Barney. "At this stage he's just a suspect, but I'd be extremely grateful for any help you could offer."

Granny put a hand on Boris. "Hold it right there, Boris. Don't say anything that will implicate you. I know how the police work." She looked at Barney. "What do you want to know, fed? Are you trying to butter Boris up with your good cop act? It won't work in this cottage. I've been around the block too many times to be taken in by good looks and a truncheon."

"Granny," said Willow. "This is Barney you're talking to. Penelope's boyfriend and friend of the family. Show him some respect!"

"Right now, I'm talking to the badge," said Granny. "I only see a uniform, not the man beneath, and the uniform *screams* violent fed."

Barney smiled. "This... fed, let you and your goat get away with the very serious crime of arson, Mrs Weaver. Remember?"

Granny smiled. "Call me Gladys, Barney, please. None of this *Mrs Weaver* — we're practically family now, we can afford to be a little courteous to each other. More tea?"

Barney shook his head. "No thanks, Gladys. This is urgent, I need to find out what Boris knows."

Boris gazed up at Granny. "Gladys. Could this be why fate brought me to you? Did fate want me here to right a wrong? Was I sent here to help solve the riddle of the four-and-twenty blackbirds murder?"

"The what?" said Barney.

"It's a tongue-in-cheek name I came up with for the murder," said Boris. "You know — from the nursery rhyme? I thought it was very fitting as your first suspect eats pies, and we found Gerald's body beneath a flock of crows — or birds which are black, if you'll allow me the artistic licence."

"Very good, Boris," said Willow. "I'll tell Susie. Maybe she can use it for a newspaper story."

"No hack's using anything Boris says unless he gets financial compensation," said Granny.

Boris winked at Willow. "Of course she can use it," he said. He turned his attention to Granny. "Calm down, Gladys, you're being very confrontational today. Have a chamomile tea, and relax. Now… do you think this is why fate brought me here?"

"I'd be highly disappointed," said Granny. "I was hoping for more, to be honest. Something earth shattering, you know?"

Barney coughed. "This is all very nice," he said,

"but do you think we could move the topic of conversation back to what Boris may or may not know? This is *very* important."

"Of course," said Boris, "ask of me what you will, and I'll do my very best to answer truthfully and factually."

"Boris," I said, "the seer in the haven knew Barney was looking for a man who makes scarecrows. She told me to repeat a phrase to you — does half a bell, or harfa bell mean anything to you, Boris. Anything at all?"

Boris laughed. "Of course it means something to me, but something's been lost in translation. You mean *Arthur* Bell. He's an artist and he *has* been known to make the occasional scarecrow for the local farms."

"Why haven't you said something before, Boris?" I said. "You were in the vets when Mrs Oliver mentioned a scarecrow man — didn't you think to mention you knew a man who made them? It *was* sort of important."

"Trigger warning!" yelled Granny.

Boris gasped and dropped to his knees, struggling to breathe.

"Don't mention the vets!" said Granny. She placed her hand between the goats horns. "Boris, it's okay, deep breaths, deep breaths. Think of nice things. Think of brandy, cigars, and Chinese food."

"Is he okay?" said Barney, leaning forward.

Granny shook her head. "No. It's some sort of PTSD," she said. "We don't mention what happened in the vets. He's still very sore from the experience, both emotionally and anally. I'm having to apply both physical and emotional salves to help him heal. He'd almost wiped it from his mind until you brought it up, Penelope. How very uncaring of you."

"I'm sorry, Boris," I said. "I didn't know."

Boris looked at me through tearful eyes. "It's not your fault, Penelope. It's the fault of those barbarians and their glass probes. I'll be okay in moment or two. Pass me my cigar would you?"

I placed Boris's cigar holder in front of him, and Granny lit the cigar which Boris greedily sucked on. The cigar stand had once been my grandad's fishing fly tying vice, but it worked admirably as a cigar holder for a smoker without opposable thumbs.

"Is that better, Boris?" said Granny. "Would you like some brandy now?"

Boris regained his composure and blew a large smoke ring. "I'm okay, Gladys, thank you." He looked at Barney. "You're looking for a man named Arthur Bell. He lives out in the woods on the road to Bentbridge. He made a living as a mediocre artist and subsidised his income by making scarecrows for local farmers. He used my services as an acupuncturist for a hand injury which prevented him from painting, and he began relying on income from making scarecrows until the time he was well enough to paint again. He was barely making enough money to feed himself, let alone pay me for acupuncture."

"An artist," I said, looking at Barney. "And a scarecrow maker."

Barney nodded. "The green paint on the shotgun!" He stood up. "Thank you, Boris. You've been a great help. I'll go straight back to the station and tell Sergeant Cooper. We'll have Mr Bell in custody within an hour."

****

Barney left in a rush after promising to keep us updated on events, and Granny drove the remaining four of us to the Poacher's Pocket Hotel, stopping off at the carwash on the way to remove the coating of mud her off-roading expedition had created.

She parked the gleaming Range Rover next to the little Renault she'd given us, and we made our way through the beer garden and down the footpath to the *Water Witch*.

Granny hadn't forgotten that she'd invited Boris and herself on our boat trip to the pie eating competition, and as Boris's face lit up when Rosie and Mabel ran to greet him as we approached the mooring, I was happy they were with us. Mum had phoned to let me know that she and Uncle Brian were on their way to the pie eating contest, and I looked forward to a day out with the whole of my family.

Family trips were a rare occurrence in the Weaver family, and they'd been made a lot harder to arrange by Granny's lifetime bans from a lot of the popular venues in the area. Her most recent ban — from Bentbridge great ape and owl sanctuary, had even made it into the newspapers. Granny had denied the accusations of course, arguing that it must have been one of the keepers who'd left the chimpanzee enclosure open after feeding time. Even when PETA claimed the chimp liberation as one of their operations — and pictured a jubilant Granny on their website with only her purple spectacles visible beneath her balaclava — she still denied the charges. I doubted Granny could cause many problems at a pie eating contest, but it was always wise to be a little vigilant in her presence.

The contest was being held near the brewery which was sponsoring it. As with all old businesses in a town built around a waterway, the Wickford brewery was built on the banks of the canal, and an adjacent field had been transformed into the setting for the afternoon's competition.

Granny took the controls of the boat for the last five minutes of the short journey, and she giggled as she increased the power, wetting Boris with spray from the propeller.

Willow took over driving duties as we approached

the brewery and guided the boat alongside the bank as I leapt ashore to tie it off. Four other boats were already moored up next to the field, and the vehicles in the makeshift carpark glinted in the sun.

The field contained a few small colourful marquees and a low stage which was home to a long table which the competitors would sit at while eating their pies. In a small town like Wickford, a lot of people could be relied on to attend most planned events, and the pie eating competition was no exception. Children ran round playing and bouncing on the inflatable castle which had been erected, and adults drank beer and ate the pies which were being baked on site for customers and pie eating professionals alike.

The smell of food being cooked and the music which came from speakers on the stage had an uplifting effect on all of us, and Granny hurried towards the tent which housed the bar, to meet Mum and Uncle Brian, with Boris trotting alongside her on the end of the dog leash they used when Boris was in the public eye.

Susie waved at us from across the field and made her way over to join us, her camera hanging around her neck, and a notebook in one hand. We told her about the developments in the murder case, and she scribbled down notes as she listened, promising not to alert her newspaper about the developments concerning Arthur Bell until Barney had given her his permission. "Of course not. Barney knows he can trust me. Anyway, I'm here to cover the contest," she said, looking around the field. "I've just been interviewing the competitors for a piece I'm writing, they're all in the little tent behind the stage. Felix Round doesn't look too well — he stuck to his celery diet, but he really needs to eat something more substantial before he faints."

Willow laughed. "I've said it before and I'll say it again — salad is not real food, and a man like Felix needs more than just celery to keep him going. I'm surprised he's still alive."

"His wife's so angry with him," smiled Susie, "but she's happy that Felix will be retiring from competition eating if he wins today — which I'm sure he will — none of the other competitors look like they have a chance of out eating Felix. I think *I* could beat some of them. They take it all far too seriously if you ask me, it's only a bit of fun."

"One man's fun is another man's passion," I said, hoping I sounded wise.

Susie and Willow seemed to agree, and before either of them had the chance to question my wisdom, Granny and Boris hurried towards us with Mum close behind them. Granny clutched a plastic glass of beer and Mum carried a wine glass, while Boris complained about not being able to finish his drink.

"There's plenty of time for another drink, Boris," scolded Granny. "But a moment like this will never be repeated. Today's the day I get validated as a mother and get to watch my first born triumph victorious. Today's the day that Brian will bring the Weaver family name into the spotlight where it so rightly deserves to shine."

"What's happening?" said Susie.

"My thoughts exactly," I said.

Granny pointed at the stage. The competitors had begun to climb the short flight of stairs and take their seats at the long table as plates laden with freshly baked pies were placed in front of them.

His bright red suit and green cravat made Uncle Brian stand out like a clown among vicars, and Granny clutched her chest as she watched. "That's what's happening," she said with a quiver in her voice. "He entered without telling me — as a beautiful surprise. My son has risen from oppression and is about to win the Wickford pie eating competition. If any higher accolade could be bestowed upon a mother, I'd like to know what it is."

"I gave you two beautiful grand children *and* I did very well in university," said Mum.

Granny sighed. "Maggie, Maggie, Maggie," she said, shaking her head. "It can't always be about you. I'm very proud of you, of course, but you had it easy, dear. Brian has had to fight hard to smash his way through the layers of oppression which society has put in his way. Has he been burned in the process? Many times. Too many times to count, but look at him up there on the stage — transformed into the beautiful phoenix we see before us — transformed so the whole world may marvel at him. You and he are in different leagues, sweetheart."

Uncle Brian waved and smiled at us, putting two beefy thumbs in the air as Granny blew him a kiss.

The speakers on stage went quiet and the music was replaced by the voice of the mayor, who stood centre stage with a microphone in hand, dressed in his full ceremonial regalia. "Ladies and gentleman," he said, his booming voice matching his large stature. "Welcome to the Wickford pie eating contest, kindly sponsored by The Wickford Brewery — home of the world renowned Wickford Headbanger, *and* the locally renowned, but considerably weaker, Wickford Tallywhacker. Both fine ales, but only one of which finds a home in the little cupboard under my oven, although I'm told the Tallywhacker is a beer which grows on you, although, frankly, life's too short to be trying to force oneself to enjoy a beer which is not to one's taste. Drink what you enjoy is my motto."

A man hurried onto the stage and spoke into the mayor's ear.

"I digress, *apparently*," said the mayor. "So let's get on with the competition!"

The crowd applauded, and Granny put her fingers in her mouth and blew a piercing whistle. "Go Brian Weaver!" she yelled. "Give em hell! That's my boy!"

The mayor continued, reading from a small card he held close to his face. "The competition rules have changed this year after advice from the British Foundation of Obesity and Heart Health. No longer will the contestants be expected to eat as many pies as they can in order to win. This year will be a timed competition — the contestants will have ten minutes in which to eat as many pies as they can!"

Granny wolf whistled again. "You've got this, Brian! Glory awaits you! Fill your face!"

"But before we begin," said the mayor. "Let us have a minute's silence for a man whose place at the table behind me is empty, and a man who was a legend in the highly competitive world of pie eating. Please be silent and remember Gerald Timkins, or as he was known in pie eating circles — The Tank."

The crowd fell dutifully silent for the prescribed sixty seconds, and when the minute was up, the mayor thanked the competitors and organisers and passed the microphone to the compère as the contestants stuffed napkins into their shirts and pulled their pies close.

Felix Round sat to the right of Uncle Brian, and I realised what Susie had meant when she'd said he looked ill. He pallor was far too pale to be healthy, and his hands trembled as he pulled a plate in front of him.

The other competitors appeared as if they were only there to make up the numbers, with one man in particular looking far too thin to finish one pie, let alone the pile in front of him. It seemed that the competition was firmly between the two fattest men on stage — Uncle Brian and Felix Round.

A hand tightened on my wrist and I gasped as the painted finger nails dug into my flesh. I looked into the face of Felix Round's wife who pulled me close to her. "That's your uncle on stage isn't it?"

I attempted to tug my wrist from her fierce grasp as Granny pushed between us. "Take your hand off my granddaughter. Nobody touches a member of my family in that way," she warned.

The look in Granny's eyes could have melted ice, and it had the desired effect on Mrs Round, who released her grip and took a step backwards. "I'm sorry," she said, "I didn't mean to hurt you, but you have to help me. You have to tell Brian to throw the competition. Felix has to win!"

CHAPTER TWENTY-ONE

*M*rs Round's eyes were those of somebody who had not been sleeping well, and her hair was thoroughly neglected. She took a step away from Granny and allowed her arms to drop by her sides. "Please tell Brian to throw the competition," she urged. "My husband *has* to win. If he doesn't win today he won't retire from pie-eating, and the doctor has told me he won't be around for more than three years if he carries on like he is. It's literally life and death that he wins today."

Granny smiled. "Then he'd better win, hadn't he? My son has been oppressed his whole life, and a win today would show him that he's a valuable person. He needs the validation. I must warn you though, Brian can put way food with the best of them — I'd be very surprised if he didn't give Felix a run for his money."

Mrs Round scowled. "Felix would have this competition in the bag if they hadn't changed the rules. He's trained for eating slowly over a period of time, not for stuffing as many pies as he can in ten minutes. It's not fair — a change of rules this late in the game must be illegal."

"It's only a bit of fun," said Susie. "Don't take it so seriously."

Mrs Round's face reddened. "My husband's health is not just a bit of fun!" She turned to Granny. "You'd better hope Felix wins, you have no idea how important this is to me. I'd do anything to make sure my husband has a long life. Anything."

"That sounds like a threat to me," said Granny. "And I'd advise against threatening me."

Mrs Round looked Granny up and down, and rushed away. She stood directly in front of the stage as the compère gave a countdown from ten and declared the competition had started.

Granny handed me her beer and began clapping with the rest of the audience. "Eat! Eat! Eat!" she chanted, urging Brian on, who stuffed a second pie into his mouth as Felix finished his first.

The other four competitors took sips of water between bites, but Felix and Uncle Brian devoured their pies quickly, with the colour returning to Felix's face as he ate his first proper food in days.

The minutes ticked by, and the competitors ate pie

after pie as the compère encouraged them with words of support. As the crowd's shouts grew louder, Boris tapped me on my leg. "Put Gladys's beer down here for me, would you, Penelope? All this excitement is making me thirsty."

I placed the plastic cup on the floor for the goat, and as I stood up straight again, a dizzy sensation made me stumble. Willow caught me with a hand under my elbow. "Are you okay?" she said. "Do you need to sit down?"

I tried to speak, but my throat tightened and my heart bounced against the walls of my chest. Images swirled around my mind and instinct told me that the pictures I was seeing were not conjured up by my imagination — I was having a vision. What Hilda had told me was true — I *was* a seer — and the story which unraveled in my mind was as vivid as any Hollywood film.

My phone vibrated in my pocket, and I didn't need to see it to know that the message was from Barney, telling me that Arthur Bell was in custody and awaiting an interview by detectives. I also *knew* that Arthur Bell hadn't killed Gerald Timkins, and that the ten minutes allocated to the pie-eating competitors was about to elapse, with Uncle Brian being declared the winner.

With a clarity that shocked me, I saw a picture which made my blood run cold and my legs tremble, and I attempted to clear the swirling images from my mind and warn people of what was about to happen. Mum and Susie helped Willow lower me to the ground while Granny's excited chanting grew louder as the compère counted down from ten and declared the competition over.

"He's won!" said Boris, his voice distant and his outline a blur.

Mum put her face inches from mine. "Sweetheart, are you okay?" she said. "Someone phone an ambulance."

"No ambulance," I said, aware that Barney would be arriving in a few minutes to enjoy the rest of the day, and that his presence would be required to arrest the *real* murderer of Gerald Timkins — and If I didn't do something to stop events unfolding as my vision told me they would — the murderer of Uncle Brian too.

"What's wrong?" said Granny, finally noticing her granddaughter sprawled on the floor at her feet.

"Stop Mrs Round," I muttered, beginning to regain my composure and pushing myself into a kneeling position. "She's going to attack Uncle Brian."

Granny didn't need telling twice. A threat of violence towards her son may as well have been an attack on her very soul. She hurried through the crowd as Willow pulled me to my feet, and made her way towards the stage where the compère was announcing Brian as the winner and picking up the tall metal trophy from the table. Felix Round was magnanimous in defeat, and gave Brian heavy congratulatory slaps on the back as the cup was presented to him.

Mrs Round was not so magnanimous, and she took the steps onto the stage with one long leap and snatched the cup from Uncle Brian's hand, lifting it over her head with two hands and bringing it down in a sweeping arc which was aimed at Uncle Brian's head.

The images my new found gift was presenting me with involved blood, gore, and a dead Uncle on the stage above me, but Granny had obviously not been taken into consideration when the vision had been conjured. She screamed as the heavy trophy swung nearer to Uncle Brian, who had no time to cast a spell, but instead shielded his face and head with his hands. The crackle of Granny's spell was evident even above the shouts and screams of the crowd, and nobody warned her about her dementia — if ever there was time when *any* spell would suffice, this was it.

Mrs Round paused at first, the swing of the trophy slowing dramatically until it stopped with a fraction of an inch between the jagged handle and Uncle Brian's head.

Felix Round stepped forward, his shock giving

way to an anguished shout of fear as his wife transformed to stone before his eyes. The compère scurried across the stage, dropping the microphone, and the onlookers began running — putting as much space between themselves and Granny as they could manage.

My vision had shown me that Barney would be arriving at any second, and right on cue, his police car appeared through the gateway which led into the field. Seeing the panic unfolding before him, he leapt from the car and ran towards the stage, not knowing what had happened, but looking in every direction in an attempt to piece the events together.

Granny climbed onto the stage and hugged Brian as a loud throbbing hum from somewhere behind me sent the sound system into a feedback loop which produced ear piercing whistles and whines.

"What on earth!" said Boris, staring past me. "What on earth?"

The throbbing grew so loud that the ground vibrated, and the crowds of people grew even more panicked, rushing for their cars or taking cover in the tents that dotted the field.

Nobody ran for the tent behind me though, and I didn't blame them. A dazzling sliver light filled the wide entrance, and the guide ropes strained as the striped canvas shook. Barney reached my side, and helped steady me on my feet as the portal fully opened and two figures walked through, one of them a beautiful woman in a flowing red robe, and the other a short portly man with a head of gold hair and a staff in one hand.

"What's happening?" said Barney, his breathing strained and his face white. "Who are they, and why is everyone screaming?"

Mum smiled. "Don't worry, Barney. The woman is Maeve, the creator of the haven" she said, "and she's with the copper haired wizard of the west. Everything will be alright now."

Maeve said something to the wizard, and he slammed his staff into the ground, making the ground swell and the crowds of fleeing people freeze on the spot.

"An EMP," explained Mum, "an extremely magical pulse."

People were frozen in time everywhere I looked. Some were frozen as they clambered into cars, and others were attempting to climb over the hedge which surrounded the field. Three particularly brave children were frozen in mid bounce on the inflatable castle, and one old man still clutched a pint of beer in his hand as he relaxed in a deck chair, unaware, or not caring that armageddon surrounded him.

Silence replaced the screaming and shouting, and Barney gazed around the field, extending his nightstick. "Should I be concerned?" he mumbled.

Mum put a hand on his shoulder. "Everybody will be okay," said Mum. "The spell will just wipe their memories."

"Why am I not frozen?" said Barney.

"The spell will only affect those who are not magic or don't know about our existence," said Mum. "You're one of us now, Barney, like Susie is… a member of the magical community."

A crow called somewhere in the distance, and Maeve looked out over the frozen crowd, her long blond hair framing her petite face. "This is a bit of a mess, isn't it?" she said, making her way towards us, with the wizard close behind, his multicoloured patchwork jacket reminding me of a clown. "Quite a mess indeed."

The wizard lifted his staff and pointed it at the stage. "Don't you dare push her, Gladys Weaver," he shouted. "The lawman will deal with her!"

Granny paused, and removed her hands from the petrified body of Mrs Round which teetered on the edge of the stage. "She tried to kill my son!" she shouted. "Nobody tries to kill Gladys Weaver's son and gets away with it!"

"Who tried to kill who?" said Barney, his eyes wide. "What the hell is going on here?"

"Arthur Bell didn't kill Gerald. Mrs Round did, and she just tried to kill Uncle Brian." I said quickly.

"So Granny turned her into stone," I added, as Barney gazed at the statue on the stage.

"Anyway!" shouted Granny, descending the steps from the stage, with Brian behind her. "Since when does the copper haired wizard of the west give orders around here?"

"I don't go by that moniker anymore," said the wizard, looking at his feet. "People just call me Derek these days... or Derek The Great... if they so desire."

"Just Derek will do," said Maeve, winking at me.

Granny joined us, and bent down to check on Boris, who licked the last drops of beer from the bottom of the plastic cup, and burped. "This is all very exciting," he said. "But could somebody explain what's happening please?"

CHAPTER TWENTY-TWO

*M*aeve's presence demanded respect. She was every inch the formidable woman I'd been told she was in the countless stories Mum and Granny had told me over the years, and we all stood still as she studied us, with Barney on one side of me with a protective hand on my shoulder, and Willow on the other, holding my hand.

Granny stepped forward and spoke to Maeve, her glasses on the end of her nose and her face still reddened by the anger that had enveloped her when her son was attacked. "Why are you here?" she said.

Maeve laughed and the wizard smiled. "Gladys," said Maeve. "You just turned a woman into stone with a field full of people as witnesses. You have witch dementia, and you risked seriously injuring or killing a human. You could say we're here for damage control. Somebody's got to clean this mess up."

"How did you know I'd done that?" said Granny. "Are you spying on me?"

"I know whenever a spell is cast in the mortal world," said Maeve, "but it just so happens that I knew this incident was going to occur. Fate never lies, and fate told me a long time ago that I'd be standing here today with you people before me."

Granny put a hand on Boris. "I told you," she said. "Fate is a powerful mistress."

"She is indeed," said Maeve. "And fate made sure you two would meet, and she certainly had a hand in Charleston's transformation into a goat. In fact, everything that's happened since the day you developed witch dementia, Gladys, has been to ensure that you found the portal clogs which belonged to Charleston's grandmother."

"Portal clogs?" said Granny.

Derek the wizard nodded. "The clogs you found are very powerful. They allow the wearer to pass through any witch's portal into the haven... even a mortal can enter the haven if he or she wears the clogs. Charleston's grandmother owned them, and when she died we never knew were they were, until now."

"But why did fate want us to find the clogs?" I said.

Maeve smiled, and looked at Barney. "So the lawman can come to the haven," she said. "To help us with a little problem. If he so wishes to of course."

"Problem?" I said. "What sort of problem could Barney possibly help you with?"

"We don't have time for explanations," said Derek. "My EMP will only last for another two minutes or so. Just know that we have a problem in the City of Shadows that magic can't solve. We need an old fashioned mortal lawman who can look past magic and see a crime."

"The City of Shadows?" said Susie. "That sounds ominous."

"Don't be fooled by the name," said Maeve. "It's a beautiful city where the sun always shines and long shadows are cast."

"Very imaginative," said Boris. "Why not just call it Sun City, though? It sounds a lot more friendly and welcoming."

"Or Solar City," offered Willow. "That sounds lovely. I'd book a holiday there."

"Enough!" said Derek. "Please… it's always been The City of Shadows, and that's what it will remain known as. I think it's a very nice name."

Somebody in the crowd groaned and another person moved a foot.

"Quickly," said Maeve to Derek. "We must be leaving soon. Reverse the spell Gladys cast on the stone woman and open a portal, the people here will forget what happened, and all evidence of witchcraft will be removed from any of their modern recording devices." She looked at Barney. "Lawman, think about what I said, and let us know if you'll help us. The clogs will allow you entry into the haven."

"They won't fit him," I said. "They're very small clogs, and Barney has huge feet."

"Like slabs of meat," agreed Boris, looking at Barney's boots.

"They're *magic* clogs," said Granny. "They'll be one size fits all, won't they Maeve?"

Maeve frowned. "Actually, no they're not, but he doesn't have to wear them, he can carry them. It's the magic they contain that's important, not the fact that they're on someone's feet or not."

"A key would have been better in that case," said Boris.

"What?" said Derek, pointing his staff as he prepared to reverse the spell on Mrs Round.

"If you don't need to wear them to enter the haven, then it seems pointless to have imbued the clogs with magic. A key would have been more symbolic," explained Boris. "Don't you think?"

"Enough of this nonsense," said Derek. "Clogs, key... does it matter in the grand scheme of things?"

"Just saying," said Boris.

Derek sighed and cast his spell. "The petrification

spell will wear off in a minute, the woman won't remember being turned into stone, but she'll be confused." Derek pointed his staff at the tent the portal had opened in, and the entrance shimmered with silver as the portal formed again.

Maeve slipped her hand into a long pocket in her robe. "This is for you, Gladys," she said, handing Granny a small bottle with a cork stopper. "It will cure your witch dementia, and you'll be able to put Charleston's mind back into his own body and the mind of that poor goat back where it belongs."

Granny took the bottle and slid it into her own pocket. "Thank you, Maeve."

Derek gave a last look over his shoulder before entering the portal, and Maeve paused for a moment before following him. "Think about what I ask of you, lawman," she said to Barney. "Your help would be greatly appreciated and fairly rewarded."

Barney nodded. "I will," he promised.

Maeve stepped into the light, and the portal closed after her, leaving us surrounded by people who were beginning to regain their senses and stare at each other in confusion.

"Ignore them," said Granny. "They'll be as right as rain soon enough. They'll think they all got collective sunstroke or something. It's a very hot day."

"You need to make an arrest," I said grabbing Barney by the wrist and leading him towards the stage where Mrs Round was standing with her head in her hands, fully transformed back into flesh and bone, and with a blank look on her face. "Come on."

"How do you know she did it?" said Barney, following me. "What evidence do you have?"

"I saw it," I said. "With my new gift. I also know that Arthur Bell told you he argued with Gerald because he was buying electronic crow scarers instead of paying Arthur to make scarecrows for him. He needed the money and was upset with Gerald."

"That's exactly what he told me," said Barney.

"He's telling the truth," I said, "He didn't hurt Gerald. His fingerprint won't match the partial print on the gun, and I'll bet that the green paint on Gerald's gun is actually nail polish which matches the colour of Mrs Round's nails perfectly. She's the murderer, and before you got here she tried to crack Uncle Brian's skull open with that trophy at her feet. She's a maniac who needs locking up."

Barney followed me onto the stage where Felix was still regaining his composure and the compère was huddled beneath the table where he'd hidden when Granny had transformed a woman to stone before his eyes.

"What's happening?" said Felix. He looked at the trophy on the floor. "Did I win?"

"Im afraid not, Felix," I said. "Brian won. You must have fainted. It's very hot."

Barney pushed past me and stood in front of Mrs Round. "Why did you kill Gerald Timkins?" he said.

Mrs Round narrowed her eyes and rubbed her head. She still looked confused, but the seriousness of the situation was beginning to show in her eyes. "I didn't!" she said. "That's an absurd accusation!"

Barney grabbed Mrs Round's hand and inspected her bright green fingernails. "We found green paint on the shotgun, Mrs Round, and I'm willing to bet it's a perfect match for the paint on your nails. We also have a partial fingerprint. I'm sure we'll clear things up soon enough."

"Ridiculous!" said Felix. "My wife wouldn't kill a man... would you, darling?"

Mrs Round took a deep breath. She put a hand on Felix's stomach and sighed. "I'm sorry, Felix," she said.

"Why did you kill him?" said Barney, taking his handcuffs from his belt.

Mrs Round looked at me swallowed hard. She turned her gaze to Barney. "It was an accident," she said, her voice low. "I went to see Gerald to beg him to withdraw from the pie-eating competition so Felix would win. I was so scared about Felix's health, I wasn't thinking straight. Gerald was in his field and his gun was on the ground, and I just picked it up. I had no idea it would go off, I just wanted to scare him."

"But you killed him instead," said Barney. "And left him there for his wife to find."

Mrs Round sobbed. "It was an accident and I couldn't allow myself to be caught — if I'd gone to prison who would have looked after Felix? He'd have eaten himself into an early grave with me not around to control him."

Felix gasped. "You killed Gerald Timkins. How could you?"

"And why did you attack my son?" said Granny, joining us on stage and peering over her glasses.

"I lost control," said Mrs Round. "All the years of watching Felix get fatter and fatter, and more ill, took their toll on me. Today was the day I thought Felix would stop. I thought that if he won today he'd never enter another competition — he promised me he'd retire if he beat Gerald's record, and I believed him. When Brian won, I lost my temper. I'm so ashamed."

"Well, you'll have a long time to come to terms with what you've done," said Granny. "In prison."

Mrs Round stumbled, and Barney caught her. "Who will look after Felix?" she said. "He won't be able to help himself when I'm locked away, he'll eat himself to death."

"I can look after myself," said Felix. "And don't you dare use me as the reason you murdered a man. That's not fair." He turned to Barney. "Take her away, officer. I can't look at her again."

The clinking sound of handcuffs being locked brought home the reality of what she'd done, and Mrs Round sobbed loudly as Barney led her from the stage and to the waiting police car.

GRANNY AND BORIS sat together on the grass near the water's edge, and Willow, Susie, and I sat at the picnic bench, listening to the radio and drinking wine. Mabel sat at our feet, and Rosie was curled up on the roof of the *Water Witch,* enjoying the last of the evening sun.

Barney had telephoned to tell us that Mrs Round had made a full confession and that her fingerprint matched the partial print on the gun, and Arthur Bell had been released from custody with an apology.

All in all, it had been a good day. Susie had got a scoop for the newspaper, Barney had arrested a murderer and been invited to the haven, and I'd had my first vision. The only thing we couldn't understand was why Granny hadn't immediately taken the cure for witch dementia that Maeve had given her.

Boris and Granny had excused themselves from our company and had been speaking in hushed tones for at least twenty minutes, but finally they both got to their feet and joined us at the table, with Boris standing next to granny as she pushed onto the bench beside me.

"We've come to a decision," said Granny.

"A joint decision," said Boris.

"Yes?" said Willow.

Granny sighed. "Today my witch dementia nearly got my son killed when my spells got muddled up."

"Erm… what are you talking about?" I said. "The spell you cast was perfect — it stopped Mrs Round in her tracks. Literally."

"You don't understand," said Granny. "That was an accident. I was trying to turn her heart to charcoal. She would have died on the spot — *should* have died on the spot — nobody tries to kill my son. Nobody! Nobody! Nobody!"

"There, there, Gladys," said Boris. "Keep it real. Think happy thoughts."

Granny shifted her weight and cleared her throat. "My apologies. I didn't mean to shout. As I was saying — today a near catastrophe happened because of my dementia, and I know I need to cure it, but…"

"But what?" I said.

Granny continued. "But, I've — I mean *Boris and I* have decided, that I won't cure it for another few weeks. Boris and I have a holiday booked, you see. In Wales — we've booked a beautiful static caravan for the week and we're looking forward to going. As soon as I drink that potion Maeve gave me, I'll be cured, and all my mistakes will be righted — which means Boris and Charleston will swap places immediately. That goose will turn back into a real bird too — all manner of little things might happen."

"That's good though isn't it?" said Susie. She looked at Boris. "You want your old life back, don't you?"

"Truth be told," said Boris, "not just yet. I'm happy, and as Gladys said — we want to go on holiday, and we've paid for one adult and one well behaved pet. That's me by the way."

"I'm sure they mean dogs," I said. "Not goats."

"Well *they* should check their small print in the brochure," said Granny. "It says *pets* not *dogs*, and anyway, Boris is far more well behaved than any dog could ever be."

Boris puffed out his chest. "I try my best," he said.

"You could go as Charleston, Boris," said Willow. "You could go on the holiday in your human body."

Granny sucked in air and shuddered. "Share a caravan with another man! Norman would turn in his grave. Rest his soul. No, Boris and I will go as we are. We're driving to Wales in the Range Rover next week, and we're going to have a wonderfully restful holiday. When we get back we'll further discuss curing my dementia."

"And find out what favour Maeve wants from Barney," said Susie.

Willow nodded. "Imagine what we can do with those clogs. Maeve said any mortal can get into the haven with them, so that means you can go too, Susie, and me — even if I haven't got my entry spell. We can all go to the City of Shadows. Together. It'll be an adventure!"

"Do you think Barney will agree to go?" said Susie. "He looked a little terrified today to be honest. I don't think he's processed the whole magic thing very well yet."

"He's not used to it, Susie," I said. "He's only known that magic exists for a few days, you've known for twelve years. I think he's doing very well, and I'm sure he'll be happy to come to the haven."

"You'll find out soon enough," said Granny. "If Maeve and the copper haired — I mean *Derek,* think it's fate that led us all to where we are today, then I can only imagine that the favour they want from Barney is a big one. Fate wouldn't interfere in trivial matters."

I sipped my wine and smiled. "Well, let's wait and see what fate has in store for us next," I said. "I can't wait to find out."

The End

ABOUT THE AUTHOR

Sam Short loves witches, goats, and narrowboats. He really enjoys writing fiction that makes him laugh — in the hope it will make others laugh too!

Printed in Great Britain
by Amazon